I CAR
YOU ON
EAGLES'
WINGS

Clare looked at the ground. She wanted to know how his mother was, wanted to ask. But she didn't want to be like all the rest – asking a glib question, waiting for a glib answer. She wanted to touch him, too, but she was scared he'd pull away – scared he'd be angry. Biting her lip, she reached out and slid her hand into his. Tony was still staring across the fields, over the grey rooftops to the sea. He didn't move. He was glad she was there. After a moment Clare took a deep breath and asked, "How bad is she?"

There was a long pause until Tony turned round and looked at her. Then, very quietly, he said, "She's the worst I've seen her."

Point

I CARRIED YOU ON EAGLES' WINGS

Sue Mayfield

SCHOLASTIC

353a

For Jonah

Grateful acknowledgement is due to
Blue Mountain Music Ltd for
permission to quote from *I Still Haven't
Found What I'm Looking For* ©1987
and *Where the Streets Have No Name* © 1987
Words and Music by Paul Hewson, Dave Evans,
Larry Mullen and Adam Clayton

Scholastic Children's Books
Scholastic Publications Ltd,
7–9 Pratt Street, London NW1 0AE, UK

Scholastic Inc.,
555 Broadway, New York, NY 10012-3999, USA

Scholastic Canada Ltd,
123 Newkirk Road, Richmond Hill,
Ontario, Canada L4C 3G5

Ashton Scholastic Pty Ltd,
P O Box 579, Gosford, New South Wales,
Australia

Ashton Scholastic Ltd,
Private Bag 92801, Penrose, Auckland,
New Zealand

First published in 1990 by André Deutsch Limited
This edition by Scholastic Publications Ltd, 1995

Copyright © Sue Mayfield, 1990

ISBN 0 590 55939 7

Typeset by TW Typesetting, Midsomer Norton, Avon
Printed by Cox & Wyman Ltd, Reading, Berks.

10 9 8 7 6 5 4 3 2 1

Chapter 1

The tide was well out this morning and the wet stretch of sand was pale and crinkly in the thin sunlight. A pair of oyster catchers were poking in the shallows, red twiglet legs and bobbing heads, worrying at the sand with their beaks.

Tony stood on the cliff watching the birds, blowing on his fingers to warm them. He liked the early morning, liked to be quiet and alone. The luminous green sack slung across his shoulder was light now. He turned along the seafront, slipped his last bundle – a *Daily Mail* and *The People's Friend* – through Mrs Ferguson's at number 47, and headed for home.

Hopping over the wall, he cut through the

churchyard, past the familiar, mossy tombstones. There was one stone that had haunted him as a child – a great blackened column with a carved eagle hunched over the top, like some hideous vulture waiting to swoop. He knew the inscription by heart.

Kicking a Coke can with a stylish left-footer he jumped down into the vicarage garden. Football practice this lunchtime … mustn't forget his kit … and money for the trip … last day for paying for the trip to the Natural History Museum …

Dad was in the kitchen, making toast.

"Morning, son," he said, as Tony came in kicking off his trainers.

"It's freezing out there." Tony flicked the switch on the kettle. "Where's Mum?" he said.

"She's tired – she thought she'd stay in bed till after breakfast today – Betty can get her up when she arrives. I'm out all morning – I've got two funerals to do at the crem then I'm popping in to the drop-in centre to see how it's going. Will you be here for lunch?"

"No, it's football practice … and, Dad, can I have £1.50 for the museum trip?"

His dad nodded as he bit into a slice of toast and marmalade. Tony crossed to the shelf and rummaged in an old golden syrup tin that was wedged between the coffee jar and a box of biscuits. He shook some coins on to the bench and counted out one pound fifty.

"Is Mum awake?"

"I think so."

"I'll take her her breakfast."

Tony's mum was lying flat on her back with her eyes closed as he opened the door. The shape of her body under the bedclothes, and the way she clasped one hand in the other on top of the sheets, made her look, Tony thought, like the statue of a saint he'd once seen in a cathedral, lying marble and tranquil on the top of a tomb. He kissed his mother's forehead and she opened her eyes and smiled weakly.

"I've brought you your breakfast. Shall I sit you up?" His mum nodded.

"Three notches or four?"

"Four, please, and mind your back."

Tony pulled the special lever behind his mother's pillow and cranked up the headrest till she was in a sitting position. He arranged the pillows behind her head and slipped the tray in front of her. As he spooned mouthfuls of well-soaked Weetabix he told her about the oyster catchers and about football practice and the trip to the Natural History Museum.

"Mr Craven says there's a big collection of stuffed birds ... lots of albatrosses and puffins and things. You never know, there might even be an eagle."

He winked at his mother. She smiled and squeezed his hand.

"Tony, it's 8.30." His dad's voice came from the stairs. He'd be late. He was late already in fact. He hated being late, hated the embarrassment of walking in to Assembly when everyone was seated and quiet – hated being treated as different.

"What about your tea?"

His mother's tea stood untouched on the Newcastle United tray. He'd carefully made it for her – weak with lots of milk to cool it down, so it looked a dirty white colour – and had poured it into her plastic feeder cup with a lid. He knew unless he helped her she wouldn't drink it. Her hands were too shaky to lift things accurately to her mouth and she hated to spill on the covers.

"Leave it. You'll be late," she said. Tony kissed her cheek and waved as he left the room.

"I hope you score," she called after him faintly, but he was out of earshot.

Assembly had started when Tony arrived. Mr Mitchell the deputy head was lecturing Year Ten about spitting on the pavement outside school. Four rows of heads turned to stare as Tony slipped in. His form teacher, Mr Jones, nodded to him and mouthed, "All right?" Tony flashed him a half smile and slumped down in his chair. The lecture ground on and then two mumbling sixth-formers read something about pollution and protecting the environment. Tony wasn't really listening. He was wondering how to cover up the fact that he'd forgotten to do his maths homework and was staring at the dandruff on the back of Danny Mason's blazer. The deputy head dismissed them and there was a rumble of conversation and coughing.

"Leave the hall with*out* talking, Year Ten!" bellowed a voice.

"Since when have lapel badges been school uniform, Sharp?" growled Mr Mitchell as he passed Tony in the corridor on the way from the hall. Tony jumped and blushed.

"Don't know, sir," he muttered.

"U2. Is that some sort of political statement, Sharp?"

"No, sir. It's a band."

"A band, Sharp," Mitchell continued with a smug nod. "What, a brass band?"

"No, sir, a rock band." Tony squirmed.

"Well, band or no band, your badge is now banned, ha-ha." Mitchell chuckled to himself. "Come and get it from my office at four o'clock, and don't let's see it in school again."

Tony fumbled at his jacket and, unpinning the badge, handed it over. He was flustered and annoyed. Mitchell had a way of making you feel about two inches tall and of making you blush, and stammer, and sound like an idiot.

"I didn't know you liked U2." Clare Sunderland was alongside him. Tony was surprised and blurted out, "Yeah."

"So do I," she said. She turned up the stairs to the science lab and was gone. He was pleased she'd spoken to him – it made him feel sort of warm and nice – but embarrassed too. Clare must have seen him red and fumbling in front of Mitchell. Mitchell was a swine: he prowled the corridors all day long, looking for red socks and lapel badges and earrings and girls with too much lipstick. There were always rows of kids outside his office at hometime, queueing up for their jewellery, or their coats that weren't the right regulation blue. Tony was annoyed about his badge. He'd only bought it at the weekend. He'd been to see a film of a U2 concert – been up to Newcastle on the train – spent his birthday money on it – bought an album, and a T-shirt, and two badges. He thought U2 were brilliant. Someone at school had once said Tony looked a bit like Bono. He'd been trying to grow his hair long ever since, but his dad kept telling him it looked a mess and making him get it cut …

"Shouldn't you be in maths?" Mr Jones put a hand on Tony's shoulder.

"Sorry, I was miles away," said Tony, realizing he'd been standing at the bottom of the stairs since Clare had run up them.

"So I see! How's your mum?" Mr Jones looked earnestly into Tony's eyes as he said this and Tony looked away, feeling his gaze as an intrusion. Why must he always be so damned sincere and concerned? Tony was embarrassed by the teacher's questions. Sure, he cared – and he was a nice enough guy – but that question, "How's your mum?" all the time – and the tender pats on the shoulder. Tony wanted to back off. It was as if Mr Jones wanted him to open up, to tell him everything he was thinking, to show his feelings, to cry even – he couldn't handle that, it made him uncomfortable. Tony pulled away.

"She's fine," he answered quickly, and he went to maths.

Chapter 2

"God, that was a jammy goal, Tones!" Gary Stevens planted a muddy football boot on Tony's backside and knocked him off balance.

"Was it heck jammy, just sheer skill!" Tony reeled round and shoved Gary sideways.

"I've seen more skill in a jam sandwich," Gary taunted. Tony laughed and flicked two fingers at Gary.

"Oh, Tony Sharp! And you a vicar's kid!"

The two of them grinned and walked together to the changing room.

Tony was sweating and very dirty. It was drizzling and he was soaked through. His legs had gone a funny blue colour with the cold. He was pleased with his performance, despite the lucky goal.

"Good game, Tony. I hope you'll play like that on Monday." Mr Craven, the team coach, patted Tony on the back as he peeled off his sodden shirt.

"Teacher's pet!" smirked Gary.

Tony took a hot shower and dressed quickly. As he stood combing his hair in the mirror, he stroked his top lip. A band of dark hair was just starting to show. He squeezed a blackhead on his chin just as the bell went for the afternoon's lessons.

"Ugh! Disgusting!" said Gary as he jostled Tony out into the corridor.

"See you in Food Technology," he shouted as he ran up the stairs.

It was three o'clock and the afternoon was dragging by slowly. Tony was sucking the tooth-marked end of his Biro and staring at a wallchart about removing stains from clothing. There was a cartoon of a woman holding up a pair of grass-stained shorts and looking desperate and a friendly box of biological powder, with arms and legs, and a smile, jumping out to save the day. The room was warm. Tony was wedged between a cooker and the radiator, leaning his elbows on the table top. The exertion of the lunchtime football, the hot shower, and now the cosy classroom, made him feel very sleepy. He noticed Danny Mason on the other side of the room rolling pieces of file paper into tiny balls and flicking them across the desk.

Miss Bridgewater was talking about cleaning

ovens and was writing "Five Steps To Cleaning Your Oven" on the blackboard.

"Right, Year Ten, I'd like you to write down this heading on a clean sheet of file paper and make notes from chapter thirteen of *Maintaining a Household*, but before you do that, let's see how much you know already. Danny, how would you clean an oven?"

"*I* don't know!" Danny looked defensive, as though there was no earthly reason why he should know.

"Haven't you ever cleaned an oven?" the teacher continued.

"No."

"So who cleans the oven in your house?"

"Me mam, who d'ya think?"

Clare Sunderland was sitting at the desk opposite. She sat up very straight and said, "Why should your mum do it?"

Danny was caught off-guard. " 'Cos it's a woman's job," he said, hoping to silence her.

"Why is it?" Clare wasn't going to be put off.

Danny looked away and said with contempt, "Huh! I wouldn't marry you!"

"You wouldn't be *asked*!" Clare flounced round in her chair with a look of triumph.

"Bloody slag ..." muttered Danny.

"We'll have less of that language, Danny. Right, who *has* cleaned an oven...?"

Tony watched all this with some delight. He didn't like Danny much. He was a big-mouth, always throwing his weight around. For some reason that Tony could never quite understand lots of girls seemed to fancy Danny and he'd been out with half the girls in Year Nine, if what he said was anything to go by. Tony liked Clare, too, though he was a bit in awe of her. She was different from the rest – sort of self-possessed, confident, sure of herself. She had opinions about things and didn't seem to mind what people thought of her. Most of his friends didn't like her. They thought she was stuck-up, weird, tight even. She didn't seem interested in the boys the way most of the girls were – didn't flirt, didn't wear make-up, or try to impress them. Tony thought she was pretty, in an unusual sort of way – fresh, and lively-looking. He remembered what she'd said to him that morning in the corridor and smiled to himself.

Eventually, the bell went and Tony shoved his file into his sports bag. Gary punched him in the back.

"Are you walking home?"

Tony nodded.

Clare brushed past him at the door. "Don't forget your badge," she said, and smiled at him.

"She's very friendly, Tones." Gary winked exaggeratedly and dug Tony in the ribs.

"Ssh," said Tony, going pink and changing the

subject quickly. "Wait for me. I've got to see Mitchell."

Gary was slouched by the school gates kicking the ground with his toe when Tony caught up with him.

"God, you've been a long time," he complained.

"What a damned queue, just to get a stupid badge back – sorry. Thanks for waiting."

They set off across the playing fields that sloped down towards the sea. The sea was just visible, a steel band of grey, stretched taut across a row of rooftops. It had stopped raining now but was bitterly cold. Tony pulled his parka up round his ears and swapped his sports bag into the other hand, thrusting blue knuckles into his pocket to warm them through.

"God, it's freezing," said Gary.

They were an unlikely pair of friends, Gary and Tony. They had little in common, except football, but they lived near each other and had been walking to and from school together since they started at John Miller High.

"Do you reckon she fancies you, then?"

"Who?" said Tony.

"Clare, stupid!"

"Hardly," said Tony, hoping Gary would drop the subject.

"Do you fancy *her*?" Gary was as subtle as ever.

"I haven't really thought about it." Tony was unconvincing.

"Liar! She's not *my* type. Bit of a Women's Libber. Now what about Sharon Johnson – God, isn't she gorgeous? What a nice bum she's got ..."

"Gary, do you have to be so crude?"

"Sorry, I forgot. Vicars' kids don't think about things like that ..."

"Ho-ho!" said Tony sarcastically.

They were outside Gary's house. "Want a coffee?"

"Yeah, okay."

Gary's mum was in the kitchen. She was cooking the tea, wearing fluffy pink slippers. Gary slung his sports bag down on the lino and said, "Two coffees, please."

"Cheeky beggar!" said Mrs Stevens. "Hello, Tony. Your mum all right?"

"Fine, thanks." Tony didn't even think as he said it, the response was so automatic. Mrs Stevens was unzipping Gary's bag and emptying muddy football gear into the washing machine.

They sat down in the lounge and Gary switched on the telly.

"Oh, goody! Your favourite, Tones – Fireman Sam!"

Gary's dad opened the door and came in, half-dressed, rubbing his eyes.

"Make us a coffee, Carol," he yelled to Gary's

13

mum. Mr Stevens worked nights as a security officer at the docks and slept during the day.

"All right, lads?" he said, as he flopped into an armchair. Mrs Stevens appeared, carrying a tray of coffee and a tin of biscuits, then she hurried back to a pan of frying onions.

Tony always felt a bit uneasy at Gary's house the way his mum did everything. She was always fussing round, seeing that they had all they needed, while Gary and his dad sat down and watched the telly or ate. Tony was so used to looking after himself that he felt a bit at a loose end not helping. He was a bit envious too, though. It must be nice to be looked after – to have a mum in pink slippers to wash your football strip and cook your tea – to be pampered, just a bit.

Tony drank the last drops of his coffee and took the empty cup into the kitchen.

"Can I wash up, Mrs Stevens?"

"Don't be daft, lad. Go and sit down."

"He'll make someone a lovely wife, don't you think, Mam?" Gary shouted from the lounge.

"Don't you be so bloody rude – pardon my language, Tony – you could do with being a bit more useful around the place yourself Gary."

"What d'ya mean," yelled Gary, "I know how to clean an oven in five easy steps!"

"Chance would be a fine thing!" said his mum, with a laugh.

Tony picked up his bag to leave.

"I'd better get home now. See you tomorrow, Gary."

"Yeah, sod off!" said Gary, jokingly.

It was raining again and nearly dark. Tony pulled his hood up and sprinted across the road into the churchyard. Zigzagging through the wet gravestones, he vaulted the wall and slipped in the back door.

Chapter 3

"That big one's a lesser black-backed gull," said Gary, knowledgeably.

"Is it heck! Black-backeds have got yellow legs," Tony corrected him.

"Well, what's this one, then?"

"Guillemot."

"God, how d'you spell that?"

They were standing in front of an array of glass cases painted with scenes of cliffs and sand dunes and pebbly beaches, and filled with stuffed birds. Gary held a clip-board with a scruffy worksheet attached to it. They were doing the museum nature quiz which involved matching up the exhibits with the descriptions on their sheet. Gary had paired himself with Tony since Tony claimed to be something of an expert.

"Birds aren't really my scene ... unless they look like Sharon Johnson!" he'd announced to the group – twice, to make sure they all heard. Sharon had stuck her tongue out and Clare had muttered something inaudible with the word "sexist" in it.

Tony took the clipboard from him. "What a mess! Did you have to doodle all over the sheet?"

Tony had enjoyed the trip, despite being stuck with Gary's stupid comments all afternoon. He liked looking at the birds and animals – seeing if he could identify them without looking at the tags, and then reading all the blurb, to find out what they ate and where they lived. He'd been less impressed by the endless cases of beetles and bugs – there was something rather dull about insects – but there had been some good fossils and a brilliant fibreglass reconstruction of a dinosaur.

"God, look at the size of that thing!" Tony turned round to see what Gary was making a fuss about now. Gary was looking at a large case suspended high on the wall above the stairs. In it was a golden eagle, against a faded mountain scene. It was in full flight – the wingspan was enormous – a good ten foot at least, Tony thought. Even dead, and stuffed, and a bit dusty, it looked incredibly graceful with a kind of wild beauty.

Tony stared at its tiny brown eyes and its hooked grey beak. What a creature it was. It was almost god-like.

Gary had wandered off to find the rest of the

group. Tony stood looking up at the bird, trying to imagine real mountains, and sky, and the eagle alive and flying – swooping and soaring on the air currents. He wanted to tell his mum, to describe it all to her. He wanted to see it fly.

"You really like birds, don't you?" Clare was standing beside him, looking at the eagle. He was glad it was her. Somehow he didn't mind her interrupting his thoughts the way he would have minded anyone else talking to him at that moment.

"Yeah, especially eagles," he found himself telling her. He expected her to ask why, but she just nodded and gazed upwards.

"They're like a secret symbol for me ..." Tony was a bit embarrassed that he'd said this, and he started to move away.

"Symbol of what?" Clare was interested.

"Oh, nothing ..." said Tony, "... just this daft thing I have with my mum ..."

"Are you the eagle?"

Tony was surprised by this and instinctively said, "No, she is."

Clare was silent. She sensed that he'd told her more than he'd meant to – given his secret away. Tony seemed uncomfortable. Clare changed the subject quickly.

"I was going to ask you if you'd like to come round some evening for coffee, to listen to some U2 albums ... are you doing anything tonight?"

"I'm sorry, I can't …" Tony's answer was hurried, awkward. Clare cut him off.

"Don't worry. Forget it." She started to move away but Tony followed her.

"I can't tonight, I've got to look after Mum because Dad's going out, but … some other night, maybe?"

Clare smiled. "Okay," she said.

Gary came round the corner just in time to see them talking to each other. "Come on, Tones. Everyone else is finished and in the snack bar."

"I'd better find Sharon, we're supposed to be working together," said Clare, slipping off.

As soon as she was gone Gary exploded into a fit of winks and nudges. "God, Tones, I think you're about to score!"

"Get stuffed, Gary!"

"Don't say that too loud, you might offend the eagle!" Gary laughed.

"Hey, Tones, how about going down the field tonight for a kick about. We could watch a video at my house later on…?"

"Sorry, Gary. I can't, I've got to stay in …"

"God, Tony, you're really boring these days. I suppose you've got too much homework." Tony started to reply, "It's not that, but I've got to …" He stopped. It didn't seem worth explaining. Gary was already talking about something else.

Chapter 4

"Ovaltine, Mum?"

"Mmm, please."

Tony's mum nodded stiffly and smiled. *EastEnders* was just finishing as Tony switched off the TV, and walked through to the kitchen. He liked watching telly with his mum in the evenings. There were so few things they could do together and she found talking difficult and tiring. It was nice just to sit together in the living room by the gas fire.

He made her Ovaltine and a coffee for himself. Poking his head round the door he asked, "Biscuits?"

"Mmm. How was the trip?" It was the first opportunity she'd had to ask him.

"It was good. There was a brilliant eagle – it must have been twelve feet across!"

Tony spread his arms wide and scowled to look eagle-like. His mum laughed.

He held the feeder cup up to her lips for her to sip the milky liquid. Giving her a drink without spilling it or choking her was a delicate operation. Tony grasped the top of her head with one hand to stop her shaking and placed the spout of the cup in her mouth. Then he tipped the drink slowly until she indicated with her eyes that her mouth was full and she was ready to swallow. He did it expertly, naturally, without any fuss. As long as he could remember he'd fed his mum or helped her to drink. He could remember as a very small child, climbing on to her knee to put Smarties into her mouth. She'd been able to do more then. When he was a baby she could still walk. Tony had no memory of ever seeing her do it, but there were photos and people had told him. Now she could do almost nothing. Even her speech was slow, jerky, difficult to understand.

"Bed, then?" asked Tony. She nodded. "They've got such small eyes, haven't they?" he continued, "and massive, talony claws. It was quite fierce looking – just like you!"

His mum grinned as he slipped a blue canvas sling under her legs and round her shoulders. He clipped it on to the hoist that was fixed to a rail on the ceiling and pulled the blue cord – blue for up, white for down, red for left, green for right – he knew the drill without thinking about it. There was a whirring sound and his mum was lifted out of the armchair until she dangled in a sitting position in the hammock seat. She looked fragile and helpless like this, her legs flopping limply below her.

"Have a nice flight!" Tony teased. He pulled the red cord and slung her across so that she was suspended about a foot above the wheelchair that was beside her chair. Then he pulled the white cord and lowered her gently down.

When Tony had transferred his mum to her bed, he wiped her hands and face with a wet flannel and spread face cream from a pink pot on to her cheeks. She was still quite pretty, he thought. She had lovely pale skin and mysterious-looking eyes. Tony had a photograph of her in a scrap book in his bedroom. She could only have been about eighteen when it was taken and was leaning against a fence in a pair of jeans and a floppy sunhat. She looked lively, sparkly – sexy even – although it was weird to think of your mum being sexy, Tony thought. Now her face had a stiff look, as though she was wearing a mask that might crack. The muscles had grown weak and even smiling looked strange and forced.

Tony put the lid on the jar of cream and sat

down on the edge of the bed.

"Would you like me to read to you?" he said. He had read to his mum for years – ever since he could read aloud. First his school reading books, and easy children's stories – now, snippets from the newspaper or part of a novel. His mum's eyesight was too poor to read herself but her mind was as sharp as ever and she liked to have plenty to think about. At the moment they were reading *Great Expectations* because Tony had to read it for school.

"I'm not sure I'm in the mood for Dickens," she said.

Tony was quite relieved. "He is a bit long-winded, isn't he?" he said. "I get jaw ache reading it aloud!" Tony waggled his jaw and grimaced with pretend pain.

"I'll tell you what," he continued, "how about a special treat in memory of our beaky friend – since I saw him in the flesh today! I'll read you the eagle bit."

Tony stretched his arms out and did his eagle face again.

He took his mum's Bible off her bedside table where she kept it beside her lamp and a little framed picture. The picture was a drawing of an eagle that Tony had given her last Christmas. He'd spent ages copying it from a nature book and had painstakingly coloured its plumage with pencil crayons. The eagle was flying across a lake edged with pine trees and in the corner Tony had written the words "Isaiah 40 verse 30".

His mum often asked him to read to her from the Bible or from paperback books about God and things. Sometimes she closed her eyes and a beautiful smile spread across her face, as if she was somewhere else, dreaming of a wonderful far-off place.

Tony opened the Bible at the book of Isaiah and started to read. The words were familiar to him and gave him a strange, stirring feeling, almost as if he wanted to cry.

" 'Do you not know? Have you not heard? The Lord is the everlasting God, the creator of the ends of the earth. He will not grow tired or weary, and his understanding no one can fathom. He gives strength to the weary, and increases the power of the weak. Even youths grow tired and weary, and young men stumble and fall, but those who hope in the Lord will renew their strength …' "

Tony paused before the last bit and looked at the little framed drawing. He thought of the massive taloned bird in the glass case overhead, and of Clare, and he read slowly.

" 'They will soar on wings like eagles, they will run and not grow weary, they will walk and not be faint.' "

He closed the book and they sat together in silence for a moment. Then Tony jumped up.

"I'd better do my maths homework now, okay?" he said. His mum nodded. He kissed the top of her head, switched off the light, and crept out.

His mum lay in the dark, looking up at the ceiling. As she stared into the gloom, tears ran down her cheeks and soaked her pillow, and she sobbed quietly.

Chapter 5

Tony stood at the end of the stone breakwater singing at the top of his voice. The sea was crashing against the seawall, drowning the sound of his voice, as he belted out a U2 song. He couldn't really sing and he hated singing where he could be heard, but out here in the early morning, deafened by the waves and the cry of seagulls, he liked to shout and roar and try to sound all passionate like Bono did.

It was Saturday and there was nobody about. Tony had just finished his paper round. He'd flung the empty sack into the vicarage garden and slithered down the muddy cliff path on to the beach. He liked the beach in winter. The ice-cream huts and shuggy-boat rides were all boarded up and the stretch of white sand had a deserted look. Out in the bay a few anchored fishing boats were tossing about, and far out on the horizon there was a herring trawler.

Tony walked back along the pier. The stones were slippery with green slime and wet where the tide had washed right over them. Where there were holes in the stone walkway, rockpools had formed, full of limpets and seaweed, and red anemones. Tony stopped and bent down to look into one. He poked an anemone with the edge of a stone and it quickly pulled in its tentacles till it looked like a glacé cherry, stuck fast to the rock.

Tony walked carefully, dodging the puddles and pools. When he reached the shore end of the breakwater, he jumped down on to the damp sand and picked his way down to the water's edge.

He was thinking about Clare. It was a pity she'd invited him round on a night when he had to stay in. He wondered if she'd mention it again. Did she like him in the way Gary had suggested? It would be nice to listen to U2 with her, although thinking about it made Tony feel quite nervous. What would they talk about? What if he couldn't think of anything interesting to say? He'd never been out with anyone before. He wasn't sure what she'd expect him to do, how she'd expect him to *be*. Was he supposed to "ask her out"? She didn't seem like the sort of girl you asked out, and anyway, *she*'d asked *him*. What if she was just being friendly? Perhaps she felt sorry for him because he had an ill mother … perhaps she didn't fancy him at all …

It was all pretty confusing, but he was enjoying thinking about her all the same. He tried to picture her walking along the edge of the waves with him. It was a nice daydream. He had his arm round her and they were talking about U2. He was cool and confident and she was laughing at his jokes. Suddenly, she stopped and bent down to the wet sand. With a piece of driftwood she wrote "Clare loves Tony" … Tony laughed at himself – what a romantic he was!

He picked up a flat stone and hurled it at the waves. It bounced four times. Not bad on choppy water. His record was eleven on a calm day. Gary claimed to have bounced a stone seventeen times but Tony didn't believe him.

He turned and walked back up the beach towards the high cliffs. There were caves in the cliffs, quite big ones – smugglers' caves so the stories went. Tony stepped inside the biggest. There was a dank fishy smell. The floor of the cave was puddled with slimy water that the tide hardly ever reached, and there were piles of salty seaweed and pieces of driftwood littered round the walls.

"Hell–o–o–!" bellowed Tony. His voice

rebounded with a spooky echo and he remembered how as young kids, he and his mates had scared each other silly by running into the caves and screaming as if they'd seen something horrific.

At the back of the cave there was a high mossy ledge. Back in the Juniors, Gary had slipped off it doing a dare and broken his arm.

As Tony came out into the light and the fresh air, he noticed what looked like a dead gull tucked behind a rock at the mouth of the cave. He wondered if the tide had washed it there in the night, though that seemed unlikely, as the water rarely rose as high as the cliffs. It was a herring gull, silver-backed with black wing tips. Tony walked up to it and touched its body gently with the toe of his shoe. It twitched and opened its eyes, letting out a rather strangled cry, which made Tony jump back startled. The bird made no attempt to fly or run but opened its yellow beak angrily, as if to ward Tony off. One of its wings was spread out on the sand, dangling awkwardly at a funny angle. It looked broken.

Tony didn't know what to do. It might bite him if he tried to move it, and even if he managed to pick it up, what then?

"Don't worry, I'll get help," he said, rather stupidly, to the bird, which blinked suspiciously at him. He started to run up the beach towards home and then he stopped and shouted, "I'll be right back! Hang on in there, mate!"

Tony's dad was in the bathroom shaving, his face lathered up with foam. Saturday was his day off and he always got up later than usual. He was listening to *Sport on Four* on a portable radio. Tony perched on the edge of the bath and started telling him about the bird.

"I think it's got a broken wing, and it looked pretty hungry. Can we bring it home and look after it?"

"It would be nice if we could," said his dad, "but I don't know the first thing about looking after birds, and gulls can be quite vicious, you know. It's probably best left where it is, Tony." He dipped his razor into the soapy water and shook it.

"Couldn't we ring the RSPCA or something? There must be something we can do. It'll die if we just leave it there."

Tony's dad looked at his son's face. Tony looked childishly eager. It was nice that he cared about things so much. He'd always liked nature – right from being a kid when he kept tadpoles and caterpillars in jam-jars in the garage. He was lucky to have a son who spent hours watching gulls on the beach when other kids his age were wasting their pocket money in the amusement arcades on the seafront. Tony was a good lad. His dad smiled and washed the soap off his face.

"Okay. We'll fetch it home and phone the vet, see what he recommends," he said as he patted his face with a towel.

"Cheers, Dad," said Tony with a grin. "Can we go now?"

Tony fetched an old cardboard box from the garage and a newspaper and a pair of suede gardening gloves. He stuffed the paper into the box to line it.

"I wonder what they eat – apart from fish?" Tony said, as they picked their way down the cliff path.

"I haven't a clue – you're the ornithologist," said his dad.

"Don't use rude words, Dad. You're a vicar!" joked Tony. "Was Mum still asleep?"

"No, she's awake – I said we wouldn't be long. She'll be fine until we get back."

"I hope it's still there," said Tony.

"Well, if it's not, we'll know you just disturbed its sleep and there was nothing wrong with it."

The bird was still there when they reached the mouth of the cave – its left wing sprawled on the sand.

"We'll need to support that wing, or we might make it worse," said Tony's dad. "If you lift it round its body, I'll put my hand under the wing to stop it dangling – then you're the one to get pecked!"

"I'm not daft," said Tony, "I found these in the garage." He pulled the suede gloves from his pocket and put them on. As he stooped to grasp the bird round its soft belly, it squawked rather half-heartedly and tried to scuttle away, but Tony gripped its white body firmly.

"Got him!" he said, excitedly.

Between them they lifted the bird carefully into the box and shut the lid so it couldn't wriggle out. It cried out angrily as they carried the box up the path, trying not to jog the bird too much.

"Shut up, you ungrateful beggar!" said Tony as he stumbled up the sandy path, backwards.

By the time they got home the bird was silent. They put the box down on the kitchen table and Tony peered beneath the lid. The bird looked resigned. It gazed at him with blank eyes.

"I'm going to call him Bono," said Tony.

"Why, because he makes such an awful racket?" teased his dad.

"Ha-ha, Dad," said Tony with a forced smile. "No, because he's handsome."

"It looks like any other seagull to me," said Dad, "and don't you go getting attached to it. We don't know if we can keep it yet."

Tony put the kettle on for a cup of tea and

helped himself to a bowl of cornflakes. He was famished. He looked at Bono – he must be pretty hungry too.

"I don't suppose you like cornflakes. Sorry, mate!"

His dad came back into the kitchen.

"I've phoned the vet and he said we can take the bird to the surgery for him to look at it. I'll just ring Betty to see if she can come round to get Mum up and sit with her – then we can go. All right?"

"It's a good clean break – look, here, in the humerus – that's the same as our upper arm bone – see … and it looks to me as though it's an air gun pellet that's done it." The vet had Bono's broken wing stretched out on the table while Tony gripped him round the body and held the good wing still. He was calling out with the pain and trying to lunge at them with his beak.

"It's kids from school," said Tony. "I've seen them, up on the cliffs, taking pot shots at the gulls." Tony felt angry. What a bloody stupid thing to do – shooting at birds just for the fun of it.

"Will it mend?" asked Tony's dad.

"Yes, it should do, if it's well looked after. I'll strap it up to immobilize the wing, then you'll need to keep it somewhere where it can exercise a little but keep the wing dry – indoors somewhere.

It will need quite a bit of space and it will probably get very smelly. Have you got a rabbit run?"

"No," said Tony's dad, wondering what on earth they were going to do with the bird, now he'd agreed to take it home.

"But we could build something, with chicken wire, in the kitchen annexe, couldn't we?" Tony was determined that they could cope with the bird. He was going to make it better, make it fly again.

The vicarage was a rambling old place and there were rooms they hardly used. Next to the kitchen there was a small room, probably the scullery once upon a time, where all they had was the washing-machine and a deep freeze. They stored boxes and bits of junk in it and Tony kept his bike there. There would just about be space to knock up a run.

"That sounds promising," said the vet. "It needs to be a good three foot high as he'll be able to hop about and he'll try to fly once he's feeling better. The wing should take about four weeks to heal."

The vet took a bandage and started to bind it round the bird's body and the injured wing. He worked quickly, expertly, strapping it tightly. The bird made a disgruntled noise, but it had stopped struggling now and looked subdued.

"All right, Bono," said Tony, rubbing his thumb

on the back of the bird's head.

"I'd try to avoid getting too friendly with it," said the vet, trying not to sound harsh. "Once he's returned to the wild you don't want him to be dependent on humans, and he's likely to be pretty bad-tempered while he's in captivity. You could get a nasty peck if you get too close." He wrapped a long piece of sticking plaster round the bird to secure the bandage. Bono looked helpless and miserable.

"This will need restrapping every ten days or so, so you'd better bring him back next weekend." The vet washed his hands and dried them briskly on a paper towel. He was a tall man, business-like with Brylcreemed hair and a tweed jacket.

Tony lifted the bird carefully back into the box.

"What do we feed him on?" he asked.

"Fish, meat, cheese – he might even like some scrambled egg! – and give him water to drink, but not enough to bathe in or that bandage won't last five minutes."

"How much do we owe you?" Tony's dad was digging in his pockets.

"Oh, don't worry," said the vet, "I don't charge for cases like this – I just hope it won't be too much trouble for you. It's not that easy, looking after wild creatures. Good luck," he said, as he opened the surgery door for them.

"Thanks," said Tony as they lifted the box on to the back seat of the car.

"Not long now, mate," he whispered to the bird. "I'll get you bacon and eggs as soon as we get home!"

Chapter 6

Bono poked half-heartedly at a saucer of congealed scrambled egg. He'd eaten a plate of cold ham, some cheese, and several slices of bread, tearing at the food greedily with his beak. He was leaning awkwardly on his good wing, lopsided and dishevelled. Tony had made a temporary pen in a corner of the garage with deck chairs and crates and a folding stepladder. Bono tried to hop about but his balance was all messed up and he kept wobbling like a drunkard.

Tony and his dad were busy setting up a run with a roll of wire mesh they'd picked up from a DIY shop on the way home. There was just about enough space in the washing-machine room. They put an open box in one corner with some rabbit straw in it and spread sheets of newspaper all over the floor. It looked quite cosy.

"How am I supposed to get to the washing-machine with all that in the way?" said Betty. She stood in the kitchen doorway, her hands on her hips, looking dubious about the whole operation. "Caging up seagulls – I never heard of anything so daft! You should have left it for nature to take its course."

"Oh, come on, Betty," said Tony, "he's a nice little fella. You might even grow to like him."

"Just don't expect me to clean up his mess." She flounced into the kitchen where she was making coffee for Tony's mum.

Tony liked Betty. She was dead straight. She'd been helping them out for years now – coming in the mornings to sit with Tony's mum or give her a bath. She did the ironing, hoovered the floors and made fantastic chocolate cakes. She was solid gold, Tony thought – as long as you kept on the right side of her.

"I'll go and get him, Betty, then I can introduce you two properly. You'll need to get acquainted if you're going to share the same laundry room!"

"Like heck, we will!" laughed Betty.

Tony went to the garage, armed with the gardening gloves. Bono was more perky now he'd had some food and got a little more used to the bandage. He dodged away as Tony pursued him round the pen, lashing out with his beak and his free wing and shrieking fiercely. It took Tony several minutes to corner him and then he had to grip the bird tightly. He was big, nearly two feet long, and solid-boned. He was obviously quite old, Tony thought – crotchety and set in his ways, no doubt.

"Meet Bono!" Tony announced as he bundled the bird into the laundry room.

"Good grief! What a brute!" Betty stared amazed at the silvery bird stuffed under Tony's arm. "What did you call him?"

"Bono."

"Bon-o? What sort of name's that? It sounds like dog biscuits!"

"He's a singer, Betty. Like Frank Sinatra – well, not much like him – but never mind … Is Mum up yet?"

"She's in the living room. You can take this coffee in for her."

"I'll go and see if she wants to meet Bono," said Tony, picking up the plastic beaker.

"Oh, sure, shaking hands with a smelly seagull will really make her day, won't it?"

Tony pulled a face at her and she threw a tea-towel at him as he dodged out of the door.

Tony's mum was tired. She'd slept badly and seemed to be developing a cold. Her eyes and nose were red and she was paler than usual. She was slumped in an armchair, listening to her talking book machine.

"What's the tape?" asked Tony, as he held up the lukewarm coffee.

"Some romantic rubbish," she said. Her speech was very slow and laboured and she was wheezing a little. She listened without reacting as Tony told her all about finding the bird, and the vet, and Betty's complaints about the enclosure in the washing room.

"Next time you're in the wheelchair I'll push you through to have a look at him. He's very beautiful. He's got elegant pink legs."

"Like me!" said his mum, managing a smile.

Gary was unimpressed by Bono. He called round after lunch to see if Tony wanted to go for a kick about up on the playing fields.

"I've told you," he said, "I'm not really interested in birds …"

"Unless they look like Sharon Johnson, don't remind me," Tony finished his sentence.

"Ugh! Disgusting!" said Gary, as Bono made a messy deposit on the newspaper. The vet hadn't been joking about the smell.

"God, how much shit is it going to do in four weeks?" Gary pulled a grotesque face.

"I was planning to change the newspaper now and then," said Tony in a patient voice. Bono cocked his head on one side and stared at Gary with bead-like eyes. He opened his beak with an indignant "Wark!"

"There, he doesn't think much of you either," said Tony.

Gary was about to say something obscene to the bird but Tony shoved him in the back and pushed him out into the garden.

"Come on then, pennos ..."

They grabbed a football and walked up to the field. Gary was in goal and Tony put some nice kicks past him. His shooting was improving. Monday night's match against North Tyne High was an important fixture. Tony really wanted to play well. He'd worked hard for his place on the team, and he'd had a good run in the last few weeks.

It was one of those winter afternoons when the air is freezing but there is bright sunshine that makes the colours of everything vibrant and alive. The two boys sat swinging their legs on the vicarage wall, hot and out of breath after the game. Looking out at the deep sparkly blue of the sea, Tony felt happy. Life was going well at the moment. He thought about Clare and wondered what she was doing.

As if reading his mind, Gary said, "How's your love life then, Tones? Is Miss – sorry Ms – Sunderland still after you?"

"Get lost, Gary. You're just jealous." Tony was only half joking.

"Hey, you missed a brilliant video last night. It was a really gory one. This woman got her head knocked off with a shovel, and then this bloke's stomach exploded ..."

Tony pulled a face. "I'm really sorry I missed it," he said, trying to sound a tiny bit convincing.

The two parted. Tony wanted to get home to be there when his mum woke up from her afternoon nap. She hadn't met Bono yet. Tony thought she'd like him.

As he ran across the garden, he jumped in the air and punched the sky.

"All right!" he said in a phoney American accent, and he kicked off his muddy trainers.

Chapter 7

Mrs Ferguson's hat was made of purple feathers, overlapping each other in a sort of spiral around her head, like a turban. Tony sat behind her, watching the feathers quiver as she sang. She held her hymn book very close to her nose because her eyes were going and she sucked on a Fox's Glacier Mint with thin lips.

Along the pew from him was Albert. He caught Tony's eye and winked. He was a squat, bandy-legged man with a puckered face who'd looked the same ever since Tony could remember.

Tony's dad was down at the front, dressed in a long white surplice. Somehow, he never looked quite at home in all his vicar's paraphernalia. He had a craggy, rugged face and his wiry hair was greying around the edges. He was a big man, slightly lanky, with broad shoulders and big feet. The angelic white robes didn't quite suit him. Tony was never sure why vicars had to wear such funny gear. His dad joked about it – called it his "nightie". He joked about his "dog collar" too – said he couldn't afford a tie – or rather, he used to – he didn't joke about much now. Dad had a weary look these days, worn-down and heavy, and he seemed to have more wrinkles and more grey hair than most of Tony's friends' dads.

"The peace of the Lord be always with you," he said, stretching out his arms.

"And also with you," murmured everyone.

There was a polite hubbub as people turned round in the pews and shook each other's hands. Mrs Ferguson turned and took hold of Tony's hand with cool lavender fingers.

"Peace be with you," she said, looking at him with watery eyes. She squeezed his fingers in a cold grip, and Tony looked away and muttered, "and with you."

Albert shuffled along the pew and gave Tony a warm bear hug. He smelt of pipe tobacco and hair oil. When Tony was small they'd had this ritual where, during this bit of the service, Albert would squeeze a stick of Wrigley's Spearmint into Tony's palm and say, "Christ's Peace, and a piece of chewing gum!"

Tony looked round the church. It was a huge draughty building, built of grey stone, with a high ceiling of criss-crossing arches. There was something cold and deathly about it despite its familiarity, and in spite of the attempts that had been made to liven it up. The Sunday School had made two brightly coloured banners out of scraps of material and bits of felt. One was a picture of a fish with patchwork scales and the other was a huge bunch of grapes with the words "I am the Vine" written across it in spidery letters of coloured wool.

Tony had recently been confirmed. He had mixed feelings about this step into supposed adulthood. On the negative side it meant that he now had to stay in church all through the service and listen to his dad's sermons, which he didn't always agree with. On the plus side it meant that he no longer had to endure so-called "discussions" where half a dozen awkward kids sat in a circle staring at the floor saying nothing while Reg Bennett asked earnest questions like "What do you think Jesus *meant* when he said 'I am the Bread of Life'?"

Reg Bennett was very enthusiastic and keen. He was one of the few really involved people in the church. Out of the fifty or so people who came on a Sunday morning most were pretty old and wore an assortment of furry and feathery hats – though none quite as ridiculous as Mrs Ferguson's creations.

There were few people who were anywhere near Tony's age – only a girl called Lucy who sang in the choir and had long greasy hair, and Reg Bennett's children, who were a few years younger than Tony and a bit too good to be true. They had luminous stickers on their books saying things like "Smile, God Loves You!" and "Jesus is my Best Friend!" and the whole family wore rainbow striped jumpers.

Tony's dad got depressed sometimes about how few young people there were. It wasn't really surprising, Tony thought. Sitting in rows singing old-fashioned hymns with seven long verses wasn't really his idea of fun. Every now and then Reg Bennett played his guitar and tried to get people singing modern songs and clapping their hands, but there was always a bit of an outcry from the fluffy hat brigade, and Tony's dad wasn't really one to rock the boat.

Tony wasn't sure why he came every week. There was the obvious reason that his dad was the vicar and it sort of seemed disloyal not to come, but his mum and dad had always been pretty good about not forcing him to go, so it wasn't as if he had no choice. There were lots of things he liked. He liked the quietness and the time to think, and he liked some of the words in the service –

especially the bits about being made clean. And he did believe in God – or at least he thought he did. He believed in Heaven too, though he couldn't imagine what it would be like. He found it all a bit confusing. When he was small, believing in God had been easy – it was just as if God was *there* – they'd said "Thank You" to him at meal times and his mum and dad had read him stories about Jesus. Jesus had seemed like a regular good guy – like a cross between Superman and Father Christmas.

It was only recently that Tony had started wondering, asking questions. No one at school seemed to believe in God – or not many admitted it anyhow. Tony wondered what Clare believed in and, as he gazed at the purple plumage in front of him, his mind wandered and he pictured Clare in the pew beside him. She was holding his hand, discreetly, where no one could see, and from time to time she turned her head and smiled at him.

Albert cleared his throat loudly and suddenly Tony realized that he was sitting there with a stupid smile on his face and that everyone else was kneeling down praying. He shuffled to his knees with a thud and Mrs Ferguson glanced over her shoulder with a look of irritation. Down at the front a man called Jack was mumbling into a microphone. His words drifted over the rows of hunched backs. There were special prayers for

Tony's mum. She'd stayed in bed today because her cold was a lot worse. Almost every week there were prayers for her – prayers for God to heal her illness, or to give her "Inner Strength", or to be "Especially close to her". These prayers irritated Tony. He wondered why God didn't answer them – why he didn't do any of the things they asked. But then, maybe he did – Tony didn't know.

They were singing the last hymn. People were shuffling and coughing and rummaging in their books to find the words. Tony slipped out at the back, hoping no one would see him. He hated all the milling around and small-talk afterwards. It was always especially bad on days when his mum didn't come to church. Everyone felt obliged to ask him how she was and to say things like "We're sorry to hear your mum's worse", or "We're think-ing of you", or "You're in our prayers, love". It was nice of everyone to be concerned but it was a bit like Mr Jones at school – too much eye contact and soothing hands on shoulders. Too much fuss.

Right now, Tony wanted space. His mum had looked awful when he took her breakfast in this morning. She'd left the Weetabix untouched on the tray and been too weak even to talk to him. It made him uneasy when she was under the weather. He felt tense and on edge.

He wandered down the cliff path and sat on a rock looking over the sea. The church was behind him, its great black spire jutting to the sky like a cormorant on a rock.

He had a U2 song lodged in his head, the way a song sticks in your mind if you've heard it on the radio first thing in the morning. As he sat watching the gulls swooping over the waves, he listened to the words pounding insistently, over and over in his head …

"But I still … haven't found … what I'm looking for …"

He started to join in, shouting defiantly at the grey sky,

"I believe in the Kingdom Come
Then all the col-ours will bleed in-to one …
But yes, I'm still run-ning! …"

Tony hurled a pebble at a black rock that was sticking out of the water. It glanced off into the foam with a sharp clatter and, as he sang, the waves bashed against the rock.

Chapter 8

Monday's game against North Tyne High was a big occasion and there was more than the usual handful of supporters on the touchline. The headmaster paced up and down, sucking on his pipe and shouting, "Come on John Miller! Come on Boys!"

John Miller High School played in rather loud purple with white stripes.

"Up the Purples!" yelled Danny Mason, who was standing by the goal mouth surrounded by a swarm of girls all munching crisps.

"Come-on-you-Mill-ers!"

It was a cold evening and the ground was rock solid with a lingering frost. Tony was playing centre forward on the strength of his recent goal scoring. He was feeling good – confident and fit. As he'd jogged out on to the pitch before the match, he'd scanned the crowd for Clare's face. He didn't really think she'd be there – football wasn't her scene – but she'd winked at him in Geography and mouthed "Good Luck" so maybe there was a chance she'd come. Gary had appeared, red-faced, running beside him, and said, "She's down beside our goal."

Tony had glanced round to catch a glimpse of her.

"Suck-er!" Gary had said, punching him in the arm and running off as the referee blew the whistle.

The guy marking Tony was a huge brawny red-head who looked like a Viking warrior. He wasn't particularly skilful so Tony had little problem dodging round him, but he came in for tackles like a Sherman tank, panting and sweating.

Despite the proportions of some of their players, North Tyne were the weaker side and by half-time John Miller were one nil up. Stephen Gould scored ten minutes from half-time with a rebound off Gary's shin, a move which Gary re-enacted for weeks afterwards and which he shamelessly took all the credit for.

"God, I set that up for you perfectly, Gouldy, didn't I?" he said at half-time as they stood in a huddle sucking oranges. Gary had a segment of orange peel wedged across the front of his teeth like a gumshield and he was hopping about punching people in the arm.

"Good play, Tony," said Mr Craven, "keep it up."

Tony was sitting on the furrowed pitch, breathing deeply, watching the sun start to sink down behind the school. From the field he could see his house with the spire of the church towering beside it. He wondered how his mum was and what sort of day she'd had. Above the cliffs, in the shadow of the steeple, he could just make out moving flecks of white as a flock of gulls circled in the evening air. He thought of Bono, with his lopsided hop and his bad-tempered squawking, and he grinned. He wondered how Betty had got on using the washing-machine and whether she would still be speaking to him. Then the whistle blew and it was time to play on.

It was twenty minutes into the second half when it happened. Tony was in the penalty area running fast. He'd dribbled the ball into a space and was in a perfect position to shoot when the Viking centre back came in to tackle and ploughed straight into him. Tony's leg was caught behind him and twisted out to the side, and with a yell, he fell to the ground. Lying moaning on the cold soil, he clasped his ankle and rolled from side to side. He was aware that the game had stopped, that there was a crowd of faces looking down at him, and that Mr Craven was dabbing at his leg with a cold sponge. But more than that, he was aware of a terrible tearing pain in his left ankle, and of the greying clouds racing across the sky above his head.

"Sugar?" said Mr Craven, as he stirred tea from a drinks machine in the corner of the waiting room. Tony was sitting, ashen faced, with his leg up on a chair. His white shorts were stained green and his parka was pulled over the purple striped shirt. The waiting room was crowded with pale, uncomfortable people – a child with a bloodied nose, a queasy-looking girl in riding boots, a little boy with a mangled finger. An assortment of fraught parents paced about, growing impatient and asking the weary-faced receptionist how long their child was likely to have to hang around, and why there weren't more staff, and why they'd been waiting an hour for an X-ray.

Tony felt sick. His ankle was throbbing and his leg had swollen right up to the knee.

"Yes, please, two," said Tony.

Mr Craven sat down beside him, and slurped a coffee. He was a short stocky man with a red stubbly beard which he stroked as he talked.

"How are you feeling now?"

"Pretty awful," Tony said, and then, with a half smile, "I would have scored, no problem."

He wasn't sure which was worse, the pain in his leg, or the frustration of being laid out when he was so close to scoring a goal – and with so many people watching too.

Tony took the plastic cup from Mr Craven. A tall boy, a few years younger than Tony, limped into the room. His leg was in plaster up to the hip and his jeans had been cut to fit round the solid white mass. He was leaning on his mother's arm and she had her other hand slipped round his back. Tony noticed her fingers. They were long and beautifully manicured. She wore suede boots and had big gold earrings. As they sat down the boy leaned against her and she stroked her fingers up and down his back.

Tony felt very alone. It was at times like this – when he was ill or had an accident – that he couldn't help feeling cheated, couldn't hold back the feeling of self-pity – of having missed out somehow. He'd never had the sort of mother who held you tight and made everything better, who rushed to your bedside to grip your hand and stroke your hair. Glancing round the room it seemed as if all the other kids had their mothers there. Tony thought of his mother, immobile in her armchair, staring blankly at the telly. Sitting here, cold and sore, he realized that he resented her. He resented the hours he'd spent looking after *her*, hated the clinging smell of illness, the tear-stained eyes accusing him. He bit his lip to fight back tears and sipped his tea.

Mr Craven taught Tony Biology as well as football. He was a wildlife enthusiast – kept bees and went on conservation weekends. Tony tried to distract himself from his misery by talking about Bono.

"You'll need to test his flight before you release him – make sure he still knows what to do with his wing once it's healed, or he won't survive long at sea," said Mr Craven. He rubbed his chin. "I'd be interested to come and see him – and if I can help in any way – I've had a bit of experience with birds." As he said this he blushed and added, with a cough, "If you know what I mean!"

Tony grinned. He was glad Gary wasn't there or there'd have been an eruption of snorts and giggles. When they'd done reproduction in Biology Mr Craven had got fairly embarrassed talking about sex and Gary reckoned this was proof that he'd never "had a woman" – as Gary put it – and had gone on and on about it. Tony liked Mr Craven. He was shy and he never had very much to say for himself, but at least he didn't make a huge thing of Tony's mum being ill, like some of the teachers did.

"Tony Sharp?" A nurse in a blue uniform stood in the doorway with a clipboard. Tony stood up and felt a rush of pain.

"Through here, please, Tony," she said, and Tony hobbled after her into a curtained cubicle.

It was quite late when Mr Craven dropped Tony at home. He'd phoned his dad from the hospital, but the house was in darkness when he got back. He went straight to the kitchen annexe and switched on the overhead light. Bono was huddled in the box, pecking at his bandaged wing and looking sorry for himself.

"Snap!" said Tony, gesturing at the plaster cast on his leg. It was still soft and he wasn't supposed to put any weight on it for a few days, so he leaned carefully on the deep freeze.

The bird blinked at him, dazzled by the flickering neon light. It cocked its head on one side.

"I'll race you," said Tony, "see who gets better first – and if you teach me to fly, I'll teach you to play football!"

Chapter 9

Tony stayed off school the next day. The doctor had advised him to rest his leg for a few days. It wasn't actually broken but the ligaments in his ankle were badly torn and he'd have to wear the plaster for at least three weeks.

He was lounging in the living room flicking the TV channels with the remote control. There was nothing much on – Open University, schools' programmes, day-time quiz shows. He watched *Playbus* and a Rupert the Bear cartoon, and then he leafed through the pages of an old *Shoot* magazine. Thinking about football made him feel lousy. He'd be out of the football team for the rest of the season now. It would be hard watching games from the sidelines. He wouldn't be able to ride his bike either, or go for walks on the beach, or even do his paper round with a plaster cast all the way up to his knee. March looked like being a boring month.

He was bored already. A day off school always seemed like a good idea but when it came to it Tony actually missed the place – or, at least, missed seeing everyone. There wasn't much to do at home, especially when you couldn't move.

Betty pushed his mum's wheelchair into the room.

"Can I come and join you?" his mum said, very jerkily. Tony felt uncomfortable. He remembered how he'd felt about her last night at casualty and he felt guilty. He was more conscious than usual of her skinny legs and blotchy skin, and of the un-healthy smell that hung round her. Betty operated the hoist and lifted her into the armchair. It was the first time she'd been out of bed since Friday and she smelt stale and sickly. Tony hated himself for noticing and tried to behave normally.

"You've just missed Rupert the Bear!" he said with mock disappointment. His mum tried to laugh but let out a stifled, rasping cough. Betty pummelled her on the chest with her fist, to help clear her breathing. She didn't even have enough strength to cough properly herself.

"Bully!" said Tony, trying to make Betty laugh.

"Watch it, you," she threatened, "just because

your leg's in a plaster! And I think that smelly bird of yours wants feeding – it nearly took my hand off this morning."

"What were you doing to him?"

"Nothing! I was trying to pick up a wet tea towel that I'd dropped trying to squeeze through to the blooming washing-machine."

"You'll have to lose a bit of weight, Betty!"

"If you weren't an invalid, lad, I'd flatten you!"

Tony's mum was smiling weakly, trying to join in.

Tony hopped through to the kitchen to see Bono. He was looking stronger today and was jumping about flexing his good wing. Tony leaned over the chicken wire and gingerly took out his empty food saucer. In the corner, behind the deep freeze, he had a bucketful of silver fish that he'd got from the fish quay on Sunday morning before church. He'd gone down there early, as the night's boats were coming in with crates full of sprats, and herring, and dogfish. They were starting to smell a bit now – no wonder Betty was complaining, he thought.

Tony lifted out a slippery handful and put them on Bono's saucer. The bird gulped the fish down greedily, tipping back his head to let the shiny pieces slither down his throat. He looked very wild when he ate – vicious and untameable, and free. Tony couldn't wait to let him go and watch him fly again – watch him soar off on the salt air, bold and powerful. Being penned in made him look so undignified.

Tony closed his eyes and imagined the great white bird hovering over the waves. Then he remembered the eagle at the museum with its vast spread wings and its tiny berry-like eyes. Soaring like an eagle … he thought of his mum, next door in her wheelchair, with its metal bars and straps. It was like a cage, like Bono's pen, only worse. Tony found it hard to imagine her doing anything other than sitting still. It was years since she'd been able to move. There was a picture of her on the bedroom wall, riding a horse, suspended over a high fence, in mid-jump. His mum's face – she could only have been about Tony's age – looked exhilarated as she hurled herself forward with the movement of the horse.

Tony felt suddenly very sad, as if a great weight was pressing down on him. Everything seemed so trivial – his leg in plaster, not being able to play football for a month, even Bono stuck behind bars with a bandaged wing – all these things seemed so small, so ludicrously short term, compared with his mother's paralysis. How must it feel to be always, forever, completely unable to move?

Tony wanted to say all this to her, wanted to say sorry for minding that she couldn't be a normal parent, wanted to run through to the lounge and tell her how much he loved her. But he didn't know where to start, or how to say it.

"Do you want a piece?" Betty was standing in the kitchen doorway, holding out a tin full of chocolate cake. Tony turned round, rubbing a tear away with a quick flick of his sleeve. He nodded his head, afraid to speak in case he started to cry.

"You all right, Tony?"

"Yep," he answered, biting his lip. He took a deep breath and looked at Betty.

"Is Mum okay?"

Betty rested her hands on Tony's shoulders.

"I think she'd like to see you," she said softly, then she pushed a plate of cake into his hands and said, "Go on, Hopalong! Get yourself out of my way!"

Gary came at lunchtime. He brought Tony a copy of *Shoot* and a pile of History homework.

"Shame you missed the end of the match, Tones. There was some damn good action. God, that ginger-haired kid was a thug, wasn't he? You should have stuck the boot in, Tones, given him a dose of his own medicine!"

Gary was in one of those moods when he just talked non-stop, without a break. He ran through a commentary of the last twenty-five minutes of the game, retold the story of "his" goal at least four times, rattled through an account of the morning's lessons – or rather the funny bits and who did what to whom – and ended with a full blown re-enactment of how he'd asked Sharon Johnson to go to a rave with him and she'd said she'd think about it. He was stretched out on Tony's bed underneath a Newcastle United pennant and a poster of U2.

"You got a mention in assembly, as well. Mitchell said 'The success of the Year Ten Football Team, who beat North Tyne High 3–0 last night, was marred by the injury of their centre forward Tony Sharp, who broke his leg during the game ...'" Gary imitated Mitchell's pompous voice, and Tony laughed as he pictured it.

"It's not broken actually."

"Does it hurt?"

"Not much."

"Give us a felt-tip pen," said Gary, jumping off the bed. He wrote "Gary" in purple graffiti writing down the full length of the plaster.

"Thanks. I'll treasure it," said Tony, wryly.

It was quite unusual for Gary to come to Tony's house. Tony sensed that being around his mum made Gary uneasy – that he couldn't really handle the wheelchair, or the way she looked, or the awkwardness of trying to talk to her. There'd been an incident a few years back that Tony shuddered to remember. He'd invited Gary for tea and his mum had had one of her shaking spasms. Gary had seemed as though he didn't know where to look as his mum dribbled the food that Dad was shovelling into her mouth. Halfway through the meal, when the atmosphere was already tense, the plastic tube that fed her urine into a bag strapped to her leg had worked loose and sprayed pee all down her chair. Tony had noticed the look of horror and disgust as Gary watched the stream of liquid, and saw Tony's mum dissolve into uncontrollable sobs. Tony had tried to make a joke of the situation but his dad had had to wheel her away, red-eyed and humiliated, to the bedroom. As they sat poking at their tea, they could hear her crying.

It was after that that Gary stopped calling. Tony never mentioned it and if Gary came, he always kept him away from his mum – took him straight upstairs. It hurt him that Gary found his mother embarrassing but he couldn't blame him for being uncomfortable with her. There was, he knew, some well-buried part of himself that felt like that too.

"I'd better get back to school, or I'll be queueing outside Mitchell's office," said Gary, bouncing up. He gave Tony's plaster a friendly kick and bounded down the stairs.

"Good luck with Sharon!" shouted Tony, as Gary vaulted over the vicarage wall.

"There's a young lady to see you, Tony," said Betty, grinning round the door. The afternoon had passed slowly. Tony's mum was asleep in bed and

Tony was watching a women's chat show – lots of women and doctors in a studio discussing premenstrual tension. He pressed the "off" button on the remote control with a wave of panic. Clare was standing in the lounge with her school blazer slung across her arm.

"I just thought I'd call and see how your leg was on my way home. Everyone's been talking about you at school."

"Oh, thanks, er I mean, hi ... er ..." Tony's voice trailed off with embarrassment. He had a spot on his chin and he put his hand across his mouth to try and hide it.

"Coffee?" said Betty, brightly.

"Er, would you ..." Tony stammered.

"Yes, please," said Clare. Betty winked knowingly at Tony and he blushed beetroot.

"Who's that, your grandma?" Clare asked as Betty disappeared.

"Betty? Oh, she's just a friend of the family – she helps out with Mum and the house and things ..."

"Where's your mum?"

"In bed, she'll probably be up soon, if she's feeling okay ..."

There was an awkward pause. Tony stared out of the window at the sea. He wished he was as good at making conversation as he was in his daydreams.

"I see Gary's been!" said Clare, pointing at the plaster.

"Yeah, subtle, isn't it?"

"Can I sign it?" she asked.

She unzipped her pencil case, took out a black pen, and wrote "Clare" very neatly across his ankle. Tony tried not to look too pleased. Maybe Gary was right. Maybe she did fancy him.

"Thanks," he said, blushing, "that looks nice."

"I've always wanted a plaster cast," said Clare. "I've never broken anything. The only time I've ever been to hospital was when I was born!"

"Poor you!" said Tony with a nervous giggle. Betty appeared with two coffees.

"I'm just about to get your mum up, Tony. Okay?"

"Oh, I'll go then," said Clare, "I don't want to be in the way ..." She stood and bent to pick up her bag.

"No, stay, it's fine. I'm sure she'd like to meet you ..."

Tony was surprised at how definite he sounded. Betty pulled a face at him and he mouthed "Get lost!" behind Clare's back.

His mum was trying to cough as Betty wheeled her into the room. Tony reached out his hand to pat her chest, as Betty had, and she smiled with relief. Betty had put some pink lipstick on her and a touch of blusher. She must have been briefed that Clare was there. She always cared about how she was looking when she met someone new. Tony was pleased. His mum looked pretty and he felt a rush of affection for her.

Clare seemed very much at her ease. She listened patiently to his mum's slow broken questions and talked cheerfully about where she lived and about school. Tony watched them with an unsettling feeling of inadequacy. Why were women so much better than men at talking to each other? How did Clare come to be so confident and talkative and able to put people at their ease? His mother's face looked almost animated and there were flashes of the lively girl in the floppy sunhat. Tony thought of the photograph in his scrapbook. Clare was quite like his mum – the same dark sparkly eyes, and a few freckles across her nose. The sleeves of her school blouse were rolled up to the elbow and slightly grubby, and her dark hair flopped messily around her collar. Tony loved the natural way she looked. He had a strong urge to kiss her.

"Have you met Bono?" his mum said, grinning at Tony.

"No," said Clare, "but I'd love to. Do you like U2 as well then?" She looked surprised at the question.

"She means Bono the seagull – not *the* Bono!" said Tony laughing. "We've got this herring gull with a broken wing in the kitchen annexe. I'm looking after it. It's called Bono …"

"Oh, I see," said Clare, and then she added eagerly, "Can I see it?"

"Yes, of course," said Tony. He jumped up, forgetting the plaster on his leg, and winced with the pain as he jarred his ankle.

"Steady!" said Clare, putting her hand protectively on his arm, as she noticed his stifled "Ouch".

"I'd better go now, actually," she said, "I've got to walk the dog before tea. It was lovely to meet you, Mrs Sharp." Clare put on her blazer and squeezed Tony's mum's hand.

"Come and meet Bono on the way out."

"Only if I can have his autograph," she laughed.

Bono was scratching his lovely white head up and down on the bars of the wire mesh as they approached. He stopped and eyed Clare thoughtfully, as if sizing her up.

"He's beautiful," she said appreciatively.

"You're the first person to pay him a compliment. It might go to his head, eh Bono?"

The bird hopped away disinterestedly and poked in the straw.

"You know, at the museum, I asked if you'd like to come round one evening?" Clare said, as she was leaving. She paused to scan Tony's face for some idea of how he was going to react, but he was looking at the floor, so she continued, "Well, are you doing anything on Friday?"

Tony opened his mouth to answer but a nervous crackle came out. He cleared his throat quickly and said, "No," rather too loudly.

"My mum will pick you up, if you can't walk very far," she added, looking at his ankle.

"Thanks." Tony couldn't look at her. He felt as if he was choking and his face was reddening. He gulped noisily.

"About seven, then. Okay?"

"Yeah."

"Bye then. Get well soon!"

Tony watched her walk down the path and out towards the seafront. He shut the back door and, if it hadn't been for the cumbersome cast on his leg, he'd have jumped six foot into the air.

Chapter 10

Tony was still in front of the bathroom mirror when the doorbell rang on Friday evening. He'd been trying to squeeze the spot on his chin and had made it red and angry-looking so then he'd daubed some talc on his face to try and disguise it. Now he was wishing he hadn't touched it in the first place and was busy brushing dots of white powder off the front of his shirt.

Clare was at the front door in a big pink jumper and black gloves with no fingers. Tony pulled on his parka, wishing he had a trendier coat. Outside, Clare's mum was waiting in a bright yellow Citroen. Tony fished in his pockets for his key, shouted "Goodbye", and clicked the door shut behind him. He'd put on some of his dad's Old

Spice aftershave – rather too much of it, he thought, as the smell followed him down the garden path.

"Hello, Tony. I was sorry to hear about your leg," Mrs Sunderland said, as Tony got clumsily into the back seat of the car. Tony wondered how much Clare had told her mother about him and what she'd said. It struck him that he knew hardly anything about Clare or her family. He only knew where she lived because he'd looked it up in the phone directory.

The house was an immense Victorian place overlooking the sea on the other side of the bay. There was a big paper lampshade in the hallway and all the panelling had been stripped back to the bare wood. Tony had to turn sideways to squeeze past a pair of stepladders and a rolled-up carpet.

"Sorry about the mess – we're doing the place up – gradually! It seems like painting the Forth Bridge!" Mrs Sunderland swept past Tony into the kitchen at the end of the passage.

"Come on through," said Clare, a bit shyly. A black spaniel leapt out, wagging its tail furiously, and planted its front paws on Tony's chest.

"Get down, Marley!" said Clare, grabbing the dog's collar.

"My mum likes reggae," she said. "Funny how people call their pets after pop stars, isn't it?"

Tony laughed and followed her into the kitchen. It was a big room with rows and rows of shelves and acres of jars of dried beans and pasta and funny coloured spices. Clare's mum was standing by the fridge.

"Would you like a beer, Tony?"

"Oh, thanks very much, Mrs Sunderland," he said, very formally.

"Oh, goodness, call me Carol – you make me feel ancient!" she said, pouring a can of lager into a glass.

Now that it was light, Tony could see her properly. She looked older than he'd expected with strong laughter lines etched all over her face, but she was dressed more like a teenager than a mother. She had big earrings with tropical fish painted on them and long squiggly hair.

"Do you want some nibblies?" she said, opening a packet of curry flavoured crisps and tipping them into a bowl.

"I'll take your coat," said Clare. Tony fumbled to take his parka off quickly, jerking his arms free from the sleeves. He had a bundle of U2 records with him.

"I brought these," he said. "I didn't know which albums you had ..." He handed the pile to Clare, who leafed through them.

"Oh, brilliant, *Rattle and Hum* – I haven't got it – can we put it on?"

She disappeared down the hallway and Tony limped after her, a bit sheepishly, feeling self-conscious.

The living room had a sort of ethnic look. There were African heads and wall-hangings and striped rugs on the floor, and enormous plants everywhere.

"Lots of plants!" said Tony, trying not to stare around too much.

"Yeah, it's a bit like *Day of the Triffids*, isn't it?" Clare fiddled with the hi-fi and then sank down into a large green beanbag and sipped her beer. Tony perched on the edge of the sofa trying to look relaxed. He felt stiff and out of place amongst the big cushions and strange paintings, but he thought how lovely Clare looked in her natural environment. A stripey cat sauntered across the room and curled itself on Clare's knee, purring luxuriously.

They sat in silence for a while, listening to the music. Tony was trying to think of things to say. Glancing round the room he noticed there were lots of books, so he said, "What does your dad do?"

"He's a journalist," said Clare, rather curtly, then she added, "Why do people always ask what *fathers* do, rather than mothers – is it because they assume that people's mums never do anything interesting – just sit in the house all day –

dusting?" She sounded militant and unusually aggressive. Tony felt a little stung.

"My mum doesn't do anything," he said quietly. Clare looked shocked, realizing what she'd said.

"Oh, I'm sorry, I forgot ..." she said. She fiddled with her hair and looked uncomfortable.

There was an awkward pause, until Tony said, "It's okay. I know what you mean."

"Actually, Dad doesn't live here," she continued, "he lives in London. Mum and Dad are divorced."

"Oh," said Tony. "Sorry. Is there just you and your mum?"

"No, I've got a sister Kate, but she's away at university. She's doing Medicine."

"What does your mum do then?"

"She lectures at the university – in Anthropology."

Tony looked puzzled, so Clare added, "You know, tribes and cultures and things. She's travelled about a lot ..."

"Hence all the carvings and stuff." Tony finished her sentence and she laughed.

"Yep!" she said, grinning.

"Oh, I really like this track," she said suddenly. She leaned back on her cushion, listening to the song.

"The words are brilliant – listen ..." She closed

her eyes and mouthed the lyrics in time to the music. It was a blues song – slow and moody – about being rescued by love. The words, and Clare sunk in the cushion mouthing them, made him feel sort of prickly – nervous and excited, and full of anticipation.

As the song faded away, Clare glanced sideways at Tony and said, "What's it like being a vicar's kid?"

Tony was surprised, and replied, "Pretty much like being anyone else's kid, I suppose."

"Don't people expect you to be all religious and perfect?"

"Sometimes. When I was little, I'd get old ladies saying things like 'You shouldn't eat sweets in church, you're the vicar's son, you should know better!' and someone once told my dad they'd heard me say 'Shit'!"

Clare laughed. "What did your dad say?" she asked.

"I think he told them that was none of their business or something." Tony smiled. "He wasn't very shocked anyway."

"What's your dad like?"

"How do you mean?" Tony wasn't used to such direct questions.

"Well, do you get on well with him?" Clare was staring at him unabashed.

"Yeah, we get on okay. We don't see all that

much of each other. He's not very easy to talk to, he sort of bottles himself up. I suppose I get on better with my mum …"

"Has she been ill a long time?" There was so much Clare wanted to ask him. "I'm sorry," she said before he had time to answer, "I'm asking too many questions – you must feel like you're being interrogated!"

"No, it's okay – it makes a change from people just asking how she is all the time – that really bugs me – especially when you know damn well they're expecting you to say 'Fine thanks'. Sometimes I feel like blurting out 'She's not okay, she's bloody dying!' That would shut people up …"

Tony was surprised at how vehement he sounded. He stared hard into his glass.

"*Is* she dying?" Clare's voice was very soft. She avoided his gaze and ruffled the cat's fur.

"I don't know – I suppose so. She's got Multiple Sclerosis – it doesn't actually kill you but it makes you so weak you die of infections or pneumonia or something – but you can have it for years and not die. Mum's pretty bad. She's had it since before I was born – having me made it much worse. She could still walk up until then …"

"God, it must be awful for her," said Clare. "I'd go mad …"

Clare got up and changed the record over. She handed him the bowl of crisps and he scooped out a handful. As she sat down again she said, "Do you believe in God?"

"Do *you*?" he said, quickly, returning the question. Clare laughed.

"I asked first!" she said with a grin.

Tony munched a crisp and looked thoughtful. "Yes, I do," he said, "well, I kind of do. I used to – yes I suppose I still do … hell, I don't know!" He paused to stuff his mouth with crisps, then he continued, "My mum talks about God as if he was a person in the room – like a kind of special friend – like someone she knows. She says she's not afraid of dying because she thinks it will be like being with God all the time. Sometimes when she talks about it, it's almost like she's looking forward to dying …"

"I think death's really scary," said Clare, curling her feet under her on the cushion, "My grandma died recently and at her funeral it was as if everyone was talking about Heaven and God and stuff, and going through the motions, but none of them really believed any of it. I saw her when she was dead – laid out in the coffin, with a frilly blouse on and make-up. She didn't look like a real person – more like a waxwork or something – it was weird."

Clare swigged her beer. "Blimey, this is getting a bit morbid, isn't it?" She said suddenly, "Sorry! Shall we talk about something else?"

Tony smiled at her. He really liked talking to

her, really liked being there with her. He wished the conversation could go on all night.

There was a shout from the kitchen, "Clare, do you want a sandwich?"

Clare looked at Tony who was leaning back on the sofa cushions looking more relaxed now.

"Are you hungry?" she said.

"Mmm," he said, nodding lazily. "I could be …"

"Do you like Brie?"

"I've never had it."

"Oh, you'll love it – it's yummy!" She grabbed his hand and pulled him up off the sofa, and they went into the kitchen.

It was raining hard when Tony came to go home. Clare wrapped a bin liner round his plaster to keep it dry as he hopped out to the car. Thick drips of water ran down the car windows and made the streetlamps look fuzzy.

Clare sat close to him on the back seat and leaned against his arm. He was a bit light-headed from the lager and the sensation of Clare pressing against him in the warm car made him feel very happy.

He didn't immediately register the flashing blue light outside the house. An ambulance was standing at the vicarage gate with its rear doors open. Tony's dad was on the pavement in his shirt sleeves, getting wet. When he saw the car pulling up he ran over and Tony wound the window down.

"What's happened, Dad?" he said.

His dad's face was creased with worry and drops of rain were running off his hair.

"It's okay, it's nothing too serious," he said. "Your mum's coughing got worse and she was having difficulty breathing. They're taking her to the infirmary ... I'm glad you're back, I didn't know how to contact you. Can you hold the fort here while I follow the ambulance in the car? I'll come back as soon as everything's okay at the hospital ..."

Tony clambered out of the car. His dad sounded more panicky than the words suggested.

"Yes, sure. Dad," Tony said, "is she in the ambulance already?"

"Yes – look, have you got a key? – we'd better go."

Tony nodded. The ambulance man slammed the doors and jumped into the driver's seat. In a moment they were gone, speeding along the glistening road, siren blaring, a blur of flashing blue in the wet night. Clare leaned out of the car.

"Do you want us to stay, or will you be okay?" she asked. Tony felt dazed. He turned round and answered, "No, I'll be fine, thanks ... thanks for a lovely evening ..."

His voice trailed off as he looked out across the black sea.

"You've left your records," said Clare, handing them out to him.

"Thanks," he said.

"Are you sure you're okay?" Clare asked again.

"Yes, thanks. Bye. I'll see you."

Tony stood in silence looking at Bono. The bird was lying quiet, resting its head against the wire mesh and blinking peacefully. Tony reached down into the pen and very gently stroked his finger down the bird's back. Bono didn't flinch but lay very still. His feathers felt soft and springy. Tony caressed them lightly. Then he switched out the light and went upstairs to bed.

Chapter 11

The room was still pitch dark when Tony woke. He rolled over and looked at the luminous numbers on his clock–radio – only 6.13. He still woke early by habit even though Gary was doing his paper round until his leg was better. Tony quite missed being up and outside at that time of the morning. It wasn't even as if he was any good at going back to sleep once he was awake. He tried to snuggle down under the covers but his ankle was throbbing and the heavy plaster stopped him curling up the way he liked to.

He thought of Clare in her pink jumper, coiled on a beanbag. For a moment he felt again the warm glow he'd had as he huddled in the car beside her. Then the siren blast and the flashing blue light glanced across his mind and he felt a sickening sense of panic. He tried to fix his mind on Clare – on the room full of plants, and the music – tried to relive their conversation, to hear all her words again. But every time he closed his eyes he saw his dad's harrowed face and the ambulance speeding off along the wet road.

It was nearly eight o'clock when Tony heard the click of the telephone receiver and his dad's voice in the hall below. He went to the top of the stairs in his pyjamas just as his dad was putting down the phone. He was still wearing last night's clothes and his hair was all frizzy and dishevelled from the rain.

"What's the news?" said Tony.

Dad looked up. He had dark rings round his eyes and needed a shave.

"She's comfortable and asleep – and they're helping her with her breathing …"

There'd been emergencies like this before when colds had developed into infections and she'd had to go to hospital for intensive treatment. Tony shuddered. He knew what "Helping her with her breathing" meant. Once, a few years ago, she'd had bronchitis and they'd propped her up every hour and stuck tubes down her nose to suck out her lungs. Tony remembered how sick and un-comfortable she'd looked. He hated the thought of that happening again.

"Had you remembered about the vet's?" said Tony, as they sat round the kitchen table poking at bowls of cereal. His dad looked vacant and uncomprehending.

"Bono's wing … it needs restrapping today …" Tony explained.

"Oh, yes … sorry … I'd forgotten …" His dad rubbed his eyes as he spoke.

"Look, Dad, I can go on the bus – I'll ask Gary to give me a hand – you need to get some rest …"

"No, it's all right – I'll take you," his dad said, wearily.

Bono was in a foul mood. He shrieked and flapped round the pen, lashing out with his beak as Tony tried to corner him. When he was finally battened down in the box, he thrust his beak through the cardboard sides and pressed his back up against the lid. Tony tied some string round the box to stop the lid from flying open in the car.

The vet was in a jovial mood and whistled loudly as he unwrapped the wing. The bandage was smelly and a bit tatty from Bono's pecking and scratching, but it had stayed in place well enough.

"Marvellous," he said, feeling the bone between his thumb and forefinger, "marvellous. That's healing up nicely – another fortnight should be all he needs. You're obviously doing a grand job. Has he been eating all right?"

"Like a pig," said Tony. His voice was flat. He didn't feel much like making conversation.

"I see you didn't want to be left out!" the vet said with a hearty laugh.

"Sorry?" said Tony, missing the joke.

"The plaster!" he said loudly, pointing at Tony's leg. "You wanted one too!"

"Oh, yes … I twisted my ankle playing football …" Tony said.

"Huh! Boys will be boys, eh, Reverend?" The vet winked at Tony's dad, who managed a half-smile and a nod.

"Well, keep up the good work, lad," he said as he threw open the surgery door and slapped Tony on the shoulders. "Bring him back two weeks today and we'll see if he's ready for action."

They drove home in silence, neither feeling much like saying anything. Only Bono made a noise, squawking disconsolately from inside his box.

Tony and his dad went together to the hospital for afternoon visiting. They'd stopped off at the corner shop for a bunch of daffodils which Tony was clutching awkwardly. He hated hospital visits – hated the ethery smell, and all the tubes and machines, and having to whisper because everyone's relatives were there too. He hated the fact that you only had an hour, and you had to sit on uncomfortable chairs, and you could never say what you wanted to say.

His mum looked dreadful. Her face was white and drawn and there was a drip fastened into her wrist. Her arm was lying on top of the starchy sheets. It was a sickly blue colour and the veins looked as though they were poking through the skin. She managed to smile as they approached but she couldn't talk so they just sat, looking at each other. Tony took hold of her hand, as he often did at home, and sat with his fingers wrapped around hers. The little framed eagle picture was on top of her locker next to a bowl of fruit. He told her about Bono, and the vet, and the vet's joke about his plastercast. Her chest made a horrible rumbling sound as she breathed and she was staring straight ahead of her with a glazed look in her eyes.

Tony wanted to tell her about his evening with Clare but he felt too self-conscious in front of his dad. He almost wished his dad would go away and leave them in private. His dad was sitting several feet away from the bed, and not touching her at all. It struck Tony that Dad rarely showed her any affection these days. He could vaguely remember his parents kissing and cuddling when he was small, but now they seldom touched. Occasion-ally, Dad would kiss her on the forehead, but it was a dutiful kiss – the sort of kiss a child would give an auntie he didn't really like.

Tony looked at his dad. He seemed miles away. Tony had no idea what he was thinking – he was remote, like a rock in the middle of a lake. He wished his dad wasn't so distant, so unemotional. There was something about him which really annoyed Tony – his coldness, his slavish sense of doing what was "right". For years, Tony had watched his dad doing everything for his mother – feeding her, lifting her, dressing her, even sitting her on the loo. He did it all without complaining, but he seemed to do it without any feeling at all, certainly without any love. Sometimes it seemed as though he was more friendly towards people at church – all the old ladies in their stupid hats – than he was towards his wife.

The hour dragged slowly. They chit-chatted about nothing much – the other people on the ward, their visitors, the nurses – and they watched the silent television set that was mounted on the wall in the corner, and then they left.

Tony couldn't really be bothered to cook himself tea so he just warmed up some baked beans and poured them over a piece of toast. His dad was in his study, working on a sermon for the morning. Tony switched on the telly and sat with a plate on his knee. There was a nature programme on –

something about bats. Tony rested his plaster on the arm of the settee and crunched his toast. On the screen a female bat was hanging upside down on a branch, giving birth. As the baby's head emerged from her, she arched herself up to lick it clean.

"The infant bat may remain like this, with only its head born, for up to an hour ..." the voice said. Tony scooped a forkful of beans into his mouth as he gazed at the screen ...

"This time is crucial ... if the newborn bat falls, it will surely meet its death as there are predators all around ..." There was some dramatic music as the film cut from the bats to an eagle in flight. Its wings were stretched out, hardly moving, with its wing tips opened like fingers. It swooped and glided, eyes staring, on the look out for prey, riding the air currents effortlessly like some terrifying dark angel. Tony watched, mesmerized, as the great bird filled the screen, soaring with its neck outstretched. He scraped his knife round the plate, licking up the tomato sauce and then he lay back on the sofa, and within minutes he fell asleep.

Chapter 12

"Well, do not swear. Although I joy in thee, I have no joy of this contract tonight …"

"Hang on a minute, Clare," interrupted Mr Jones. "Danny, have you got a problem? Page 88 Act 2 Scene 2. Can you follow it like everyone else, please?"

"I can't read, sir!" said Danny Mason, smirking.

"Ho-ho, very funny … carry on, please, Clare …"

Clare continued to read aloud, "It is too rash, too unadvised, too sudden …"

Gary was resting his chin on the desk, squinting at the open book in front of him. Mr Jones was perched on a table at the front of the classroom with his legs crossed, poking his ear with the end of a pencil. He wore black jeans and an orange tie that looked as if it would glow in the dark.

"Can I have someone to read Romeo, please?" he asked as Clare finished her speech.

Gary's elbow shot out to the side and jolted Tony's arm. "Go for it, Tones! Here's your big chance!" he whispered with a snigger.

Tony didn't laugh. It was his first day back at school since the accident and he was already a bit fed up with jokes about what he could and couldn't do with his plaster, and with people wanting to scrawl facile messages on it.

He'd put a big woolly sock over his foot to keep his toes warm, and had deliberately pulled it up just far enough to cover Clare's name. He couldn't face all the comments he'd get if people saw she'd written on it, and anyway, he wanted things between him and Clare to be a secret. It was more special that way. He was going to avoid telling Gary about Friday night as long as he could.

"Stephen, can you read from line 125, please?" said Mr Jones.

"Oh, hard luck … Gouldy's beaten you to it," Gary spluttered.

Stephen Gould began reading in an embarrassed voice, "O, wilt thou leave me so unsatisfied?"

When Clare answered him with the line, "What

satisfaction canst thou have tonight?" there was a loud snort from Gary. Clare tutted and glanced at the ceiling.

Mr Jones looked up with a pained expression on his face and said, "What's funny, Gary. Can we all share the joke?"

There was a buzz of giggling and comments and a lot of shuffling and scraping of chairs before Mr Jones said, in a whingey voice, "Year Ten! Do you think we could get to the end of the scene with*out* you all behaving like a bunch of six–year–olds ... or do we have to come back tonight?"

Tony sat leaning on his elbows, his plastercast wedged uncomfortably under the desk. He was subdued, not joining in the jokes. He hadn't told anyone at school that his mum was in hospital, but his mind was full of the ethery smell, and his mum's glazed eyes, and the needle fastened into her wrist. He could hear the rumbling of her chest and the forced cheeriness of the nurses, as they hoisted her up on to piles of stiff white pillows.

At the end of the lesson, Tony was packing away his books when Mr Jones came up and put a hand on his shoulder. Tony flinched, guessing what was coming.

"How's the leg?" he said in a friendly voice.

"It's okay ... hurts a bit," mumbled Tony, avoiding his gaze.

"You seem a bit quiet today, Tony. Is everything all right?"

Tony squirmed. "Yes," he said, irritated at the questioning.

"Is your mum okay?"

"Yes, she's FINE!" Tony almost shouted it. He pulled away, snatched up his bag and got out of the classroom as fast as he could, bashing into a group of kids from Year Nine in the corridor outside.

"Mind out, you stupid idiot!" one of them shouted.

"Piss off!" said Tony, as he slammed the fire door shut after him.

He walked quickly, dragging the plaster awkwardly, storming blindly across the playing field towards the sea. He wanted to tell the whole world to get lost, to leave him alone.

He heard Clare behind him, running to catch up.

"Tony ... wait ... Tony ..." she was calling out. He ignored her until she grabbed him by the sleeve. He jerked his arm away and turned to face her.

"Why couldn't I say it? Why didn't I say it?" he shouted. "Why did I say 'fine' like I always bloody do?" He was almost sobbing. He looked away, out towards the sea, and swallowed hard.

Clare looked at the ground. She wanted to

know how his mother was, wanted to ask. But she didn't want to be like all the rest – asking a glib question, waiting for a glib answer. She wanted to touch him, too, but she was scared he'd pull away – scared he'd be angry. Biting her lip, she reached out and slid her hand into his. Tony was still staring across the fields, over the grey rooftops to the sea. He didn't move. He was glad she was there. After a moment Clare took a deep breath and asked, "How bad is she?"

There was a long pause until Tony turned round and looked at her. Then, very quietly, he said, "She's the worst I've seen her."

Chapter 13

It was good to be out in the early morning air again. Tony caught a double decker bus along the seafront. He was the only person on board.

"You're the Lone Ranger this morning, lad!" said the driver. "Where are you off to at this time of day?"

"Down to the fish quay – buy some fish," said Tony.

"What? Your mother not feed you or something?"

"Nah … it's for a seagull."

The driver pulled an incredulous face and shook his head, saying, "Well … it takes all sorts!"

Tony grinned. He sat by the window and rubbed the misted glass to clear a peephole. It was a cold, damp morning and it was still dark. The bus followed the road that skirted round the cliff-tops. Streetlamps on the promenade cast amber shadows across the stretch of wet sand. The tide was right up and Tony could see that the water was choppy. The waves looked black and lumpy and fringes of white foam were catching the light. Out on the horizon he could make out a tanker, heading for the mouth of the river, and above the grinding noise of the bus's engine he could hear the screaming chorus of gulls.

"So long, Tonto!" said Tony, stepping down from the bus as they reached the river.

"Hi-Ho Silver!" said the driver, saluting him.

Down on the quayside there were people everywhere, sloshing around in fishy water with boxes of ice and crates of wriggling fish. There were thirty or more boats hauled up along the stone piers, rocking against their moorings, sending bands of ripples far out into the harbour.

All along the quay, fish wholesalers were haggling over great slabs of cod and trayloads of herring, their vans and trucks parked up along the water's edge, amid coiled ropes, and nets, and stacks of lobster pots. Tony sniffed the familiar stench, thick and salty. He picked his way past the anchor chains and piles of orange floats along to the row of wooden sheds where people were slashing and filleting fish on battered benches. Tony stopped beside a brawny looking man. He lifted a whiting out of a crate on to the chopping block and, with a lightning flick of his bloodied knife, slit the silver fish along its length. Then with a hooked instrument, he ripped out the innards and slopped them into a bucket, throwing the gutted body into a box of ice.

"Are you selling your scraps?" asked Tony. The man looked up from his work.

"How much d'you want?" he growled.

"A bucketful?"

"What's it for, bait?"

"No … it's for a bird I'm looking after."

The man looked surprised. "A bird?" he said suspiciously, scrunching up his forehead.

"Yeah … a herring gull … it's got a broken wing …"

"Should shoot the bloody thing – never mind feeding it!" The man spat on the slippery cobbles and slid his knife through another silvery belly. He pointed towards the anchored boats where a cloud of gulls was swarming over a catch, a flapping mass of white and grey.

"Look at that lot – they're a damn nuisance – snatching the fish – making off with good money. I'll tell you," he said, jabbing at the air with his reddened blade, "Seagulls are the bane of a fisherman's life – pain in the bloody neck!"

94

He slapped a fish down on the bench and muttered, "Broken wing ..." then he picked up the bucket of offal and poured the contents into a plastic bag. "You can have the lot for fifty pence."

"Cheers," said Tony. He took the stinking parcel and walked back along the pier. He stopped to buy a pound of sardines and caught the bus home.

The bus was more crowded on the way back. A large woman in overalls and a plastic mac sat down in the seat in front of Tony. He was aware of the smell that was coming from his bag and he tried to slide it under the seat so no one would know it was him. The woman had noticed it. She kept craning her head round, wrinkling up her nose. When she saw Tony staring at her she pretended to be scratching her nostril and looked out of the window. Tony smiled to himself as he imagined what she must be thinking.

He bumped into his dad in the churchyard, walking back towards the house with a prayer book under his arm. He looked preoccupied, brooding. Tony caught his eye and raised the plastic bag up high.

"Breakfast for Bono!" he said, trying to make his dad smile.

"Have you been down to the river? You should have said ... I'd have given you a lift ..." his dad sounded weary.

"Don't worry about it, Dad. I enjoyed the bus ride."

The early start and the sight of the sniffing woman on the bus had put Tony in a good mood. Seeing his dad's lined face, and walking into an empty house hit him like a punch in the stomach, puncturing any feeling of well-being that he might have had.

He poured the fish bits into the bucket by the deep freeze and filled up Bono's saucer – at least he wouldn't get hassle about the stink this time, now that Betty wasn't around. He went upstairs and, running hot water into the basin, he scrubbed at his hands with some scented soap to try and mask their smell. It was twenty past eight. He'd make it to school without being late for once.

Chapter 14

"Do you want a lift?" Tony's dad was sitting outside the school gates in the car. It was pouring with rain and, as Tony opened the passenger door, his dad said, "You're not supposed to get the plaster wet, are you?"

"Thanks," said Tony, throwing his bag on to the back seat.

"Grandma's at home," said his dad as they drove off. Tony watched the windscreen wipers dancing in front of him. He said nothing.

"I thought I'd better warn you. She's re-organizing the kitchen cupboards and cleaning everything in sight – and she doesn't like Bono." Dad looked sideways at Tony, who pulled a face and laughed darkly.

When they got back Grandma was wiping

down the kitchen surfaces with a driven, hunted look. Tony kissed her rather stiffly. She took off her rubber gloves and tugged at her apron with a fidgety flick of the wrist.

"Hello, dear," she said with a papery smile. She was a fragile-looking woman – thin and pale – like a brittle tree that would easily snap.

"I'll make some tea," she said.

Tony wanted to go and look at Bono, but if Grandma had already registered her disapproval of him, Tony didn't want a scene. No doubt he would hear her views on keeping seagulls in the kitchen soon enough, but it didn't seem worth drawing her attention to it when she'd just arrived.

Instead, he took his school bag upstairs and slung it on his bed. He took off his tie and loosened the top button of his shirt. As he did this he caught sight of himself in the mirror. He walked over to it and pressed his face close to the glass. He wasn't bad looking and he did look a bit like Bono. Tony took a comb and swept his hair back off his face. It was dark and slightly wavy with a floppy long bit at the front. He stood back to view it, turning his head to the side and pouting like a model in a magazine. Then he combed it over to one side. He liked that less.

He wondered if Clare thought he was handsome. She'd been quite standoffish the last few days at school – Tony wondered if he'd been imagining things at the weekend when she'd seemed so keen on him. He wondered if he'd ever get to kiss her – he was a bit worried that he wouldn't know what to do if he did. He half-closed his eyes and pressed his lips up to the mirror, kissing the glass with a long sigh.

"Tea, Tony," he heard his grandma's reedy voice at the bottom of the stairs and pulled back from the mirror, blushing at the thought of being discovered. There was a foggy patch on the glass where his mouth had been. He rubbed it with his sleeve and went downstairs quickly.

Grandma had got out china cups and saucers that they rarely used and had covered the New-castle United tray with a lace cloth. There was a flowery mat on the coffee table and a doily-covered plate with little cakes on it. She was pouring tea through a tea strainer that Tony didn't remember having seen before.

"When did you get here?" he asked, scratching around for something to say.

"About two," Grandma said, handing him the plate of cakes.

"Was it a good journey?" Tony realized as he said this that it was a bad question to ask since his grandma hated travelling and always found the train journey up from Kent something of an ordeal.

"Awful," she said, shaking her head and grimacing, "Awful ... There was a terrible draught in the compartment all the way from York and it was *so* noisy. And ... there were a lot of people in the carriage who obviously hadn't paid for first class. I think it's shocking that British Rail never put enough second class coaches on the train so folks have to spill over into the first class carriages ... it defeats the whole object ..."

"You should demand a refund," said Tony, trying to sound tactful. He bit into a butterfly bun, scooping up the orangey cream with his tongue.

"Well," said his grandma, "I'm not one to make a fuss, as you know." She forced a smile.

"More tea, Geoffrey?"

Tony's dad held out his cup.

"I was telling Grandma about your accident, Tony," he said.

"Yes, poor boy ... you do play some dangerous games ..." she said, her face twisted into an anxious frown.

"Oh, I don't know," said Tony's dad, butting in a bit too heartily. "You can get knocked down just crossing the road, Evelyn."

"Yes, Geoffrey, but that's different from going looking for accidents by playing reckless sports ..."

"Anyway," said Tony, wanting to change the

subject, "it doesn't hurt much and it's nearly healed now. I'll have the plaster off in just over a week."

Grandma stared into the distance with a furrowed forehead. There was silence apart from the clink of china. Tony sipped his tea. He felt sorry for his grandma. She always saw the negative side of everything, always looked overwhelmed by worry and sadness.

They were sitting in the living room round the fire. There was a space where Tony's mum usually sat and the hoisting machine hung mute from the ceiling above the empty armchair. Tony wanted to ask how Mum was, but somehow he didn't dare. Her absence was tangible but no one seemed to want to mention it – it felt as though they were all skating round a patch of thin ice on a lake, terrified of falling through.

"How was school?" said Dad, breaking the silence.

"Okay," said Tony. "Mr Craven said he'd help test fly Bono next weekend, if the vet says he's ready."

"Where will you do it?" Dad ploughed on, ignoring Grandma's raised eyebrows at the mention of the seagull.

"Probably in his garage – he thinks there should just about be room …"

"It's nice of him to take an interest," said Dad.

Grandma stood up and began clearing the cups and saucers on to the tray, with a frosty expression. She disappeared into the kitchen and ran some water into the sink. Tony felt tense already.

"I've got lots of homework, Dad," he said. "Do you mind if I don't come to the hospital tonight?"

"No, that's fine … I'll take Grandma … she'll probably want to see Mum on her own anyway … and she's likely to be upset …" Dad's voice trailed off as he wandered into the kitchen to help wash up.

Tony crept upstairs. Being around his grandma gave him a sort of knotted up feeling in his stomach — as if his insides were all ravelled. He put his cassette player on very loud and dug in his bag for his French book. He wrote the title of his assignment at the top of the page — "*Ma Famille*" — then stared at the blank sheet and doodled his name round the edges.

"I want to run
I want to hide
I want to tear down the walls
That hold me inside …"

The words blasted out from the stereo. Tony leaned back in his chair and rested his plaster on the table, sucking at his pen like a cigarette. If his leg were all right he'd go out on his bike — just get on it and cycle – along the cliff top, down to the lighthouse and the pier – past the abbey ruins – on and on. Just pedalling – going nowhere in particular.

He waggled his toes inside his plastercast. It was starting to work loose now and he could flex his ankle a bit. It didn't hurt much any more but the skin felt itchy and he longed to be able to scratch it. He was counting the days until it came off.

He didn't hear his dad come in and jumped when he felt his hand on his shoulder. His dad's lips were moving but he couldn't make out the words above the music, so he leaned across and flipped the "Stop" button.

"Sorry, Dad. What did you say?"

"That's better … I actually said 'Could you turn it down a bit?' but off is better still."

Tony pulled an impatient face and his dad grinned.

"I don't think Grandma's all that into U2," he said, trying to make Tony laugh. Tony looked sullen. He hated the way his dad tried to sound as if he was on his side.

"Do you think you could try not to play music when she's in the house?" his dad asked. "It makes her tense."

"Well, she makes me tense!" Tony blurted out. His dad sighed but said nothing.

"How long is she going to be here?" Tony asked. He tried to say it unemotionally but there was an edge in his voice.

"I don't know … she'll stay until there's any change … so she can be around Mum." Tony's dad paused, avoiding Tony's eyes, then he said with fake cheerfulness, "We'll need her help around the house in any case, especially with you a bit out of action with your leg."

Tony bit his pen and glowered at the book in front of him. Why was his dad always so reasonable about everything? Why did he always say such predictable things, such proper things? Why couldn't he be honest and say he hated having her around too – hated the fussing, and the anxious comments, and the tragic sighs, and all the little backhanded criticisms dressed up like kind remarks?

His dad smiled bravely and left the room. Tony flung down his pen and kicked his schoolbag across the floor. Then he lay down flat on the bed and pushed his face into the pillow.

Chapter 15

The park was deserted. The little green boat-hire hut was all boarded up and a clump of canvas-covered rowing boats were huddled together in the middle of the lake. Tony and Clare sat on a wooden bench overlooking the water.

"When I was a kid, I used to think this lake was huge," said Tony. "I used to come down here with my dad to sail this little boat we had, and it was like an epic event if the boat made it across the lake!" Clare laughed.

"It's just a big pond really, isn't it? – I bet it's only three feet deep!"

"Isn't it funny how things seem to shrink as you get older?" said Clare. "I went back to the Infant School recently and I couldn't get over how tiny the toilets were!"

"Yeah, and the washbasins are about six inches off the ground, aren't they?"

They both laughed.

Marley, Clare's dog, was skirting the lake, sniffing at the slimey stones round the water's edge. Tony felt very peaceful. He was glad Clare had phoned him. It was good to get out of the house – good to get away from his grandma.

"How's Bono?" asked Clare, offering Tony a Polo mint from her pocket.

"He's doing okay," said Tony, "but he's not exactly flavour of the month at home!"

"Doesn't your grandma like him?" she said.

"About as much as I like Take That!" said Tony. "You should have seen her face when she found the bucket of fish guts! She went to get a bag of frozen peas and came back looking as if she was going to throw up! Then she spent the whole meal going on about how unhygienic it is keeping a wild animal in the house and how Bono's probably carrying all sorts of horrible diseases."

Clare smiled sympathetically. "Poor Bono," she said.

Tony pressed his mint against the roof of his mouth. He liked to suck them until they were wafer thin and you could run your tongue round the sharp rim, before they shattered and dissolved into minty bits.

"Shall we walk a bit further?" Clare asked.

"Yeah, okay. If you don't mind going at tortoise pace."

They took a path that led away from the lake, down through some ornamental gardens where there were archways and stone urns and hedges clipped to look like hens and snails and lollipops. Tony hobbled awkwardly, dragging his plaster along the path.

"Do you want to lean on an arm?" Clare asked. She didn't wait for a reply but slid her hand behind his elbow and wrapped her fingers round the sleeve of his coat. They walked along in silence, arm in arm. Tony felt nervous – he had a sort of jittery feeling in his stomach – and he breathed deeply to try not to let it show. Marley was scratching on the side of a bank, in some bushes.

"Looks like he's found a rabbit," said Clare. She sounded as nervous as Tony felt and they both laughed a bit self-consciously. They stopped to look into the square pond. The water was green and soupy and the bronze cherub in the middle wasn't spouting water from his trumpet the way he did in summer. An empty Coke can was floating, half-covered in weeds.

"There used to be goldfish in here – great big fat ones," said Tony.

"They probably got nicked," said Clare. "Some kid took them home to feed to a seagull!" She nudged Tony and he laughed. He looked at her as she stared into the green pond. The air was heavy with fog and her hair had tiny droplets of moisture all over it, like little pearls. She had a long red scarf wound several times round her neck and her cheeks were pink with the cold. She looked very pretty. Tony swallowed hard and looked at Marley who was poking in a flower bed. There wasn't much growing – just a few brave snowdrops peeping through the frosty soil.

They walked on, out of the gates of the park and along the promenade. The sea was lost in a grey haze and a thick salty smell was drifting up from the beach. They could hear the fog horn, down on the river – a muffled, honking sound. Clare was still holding his arm. They passed the crazy golf course, all closed down for the winter, paint flaking from the model windmills and space rockets. Marley cocked his leg against the padlocked gate. Someone shot by them on a bike. He looked back over his shoulder and smirked.

"Damn! That looked like Danny!" said Tony.

"This'll be all round school on Monday, then," said Clare with a shrug.

"Do you mind?" asked Tony, doubtfully. He was annoyed that they'd been spotted – especially by Danny Mason of all people. Clare squeezed his arm tight.

"No," she said. She sounded as though she really meant it.

A cold wind was blowing off the sea. They stood very close, leaning on the salt-crusted railings.

"Have you been to the hospital much?" asked Clare.

"Yeah. Most evenings." Tony stared straight in front of him. He wanted to talk about his mum but he didn't know how to start.

"How is she?" Clare stroked his arm gently as she said it. He was glad she'd asked, grateful for the chance to say something, to somebody, instead of the morbid silence there was at home.

"She's peaceful," he said. "They've moved her into a side ward on her own so it's more quiet. It's quite nice – more sort of personal, with lots of flowers and cards and things – and her bedspread from home. They've stopped doing the physio-therapy, so she's not as uncomfortable as she was – but she's hot all the time, sweating and thirsty. She can't talk much …"

Clare wanted to ask if all that meant that she was going to die, but she couldn't say it outright. It seemed too callous. She looked at Tony. He was gazing at the grey sea, but he looked as though he was far off in another place. His eyes were full of tears. Clare stretched out her hand and touched his face. As she stroked his damp cheek, she leaned towards him and very gently kissed his lips.

Chapter 16

It was a week later when Tony took Bono to the vet's. He went on the bus and Clare went with him. They sat on the back seat with the bird's box wedged between them. Bono was mercifully quiet, dozing in his rabbit straw, his grimy bandage resting against the cardboard walls.

It was a bright sunny morning. All along the seafront there were joggers and people walking their dogs and, as they passed the park, Tony noticed a workman repainting the sign outside the boating hut.

"That's splendid!" said the vet. "See … if you run your finger down that bone you can feel how well it's mended – just a little scar tissue – but nothing that will affect his flight."

Tony was holding Bono round his fat white body, pinning one wing to his side while the vet manipulated the other. The feathers looked flat and dry where the bandage had been and they were darker than the silvery flashes on the un-damaged wing.

Clare was standing at Bono's head, clamping his beak shut with the suede gloves and stroking the white down on the back of his neck. Tony touched the mended wing. He felt a rush of excitement at the thought of seeing the bird fly.

"I wouldn't let him go straight away," said the vet, running a hand over his slicked-back hair and scratching his forehead. "You want to give him a chance to make sure he can still fly all right."

"We were going to test fly him in Mr Craven's garage," said Tony keenly. "He's our Biology teacher," he added. The vet nodded thoughtfully.

"It might be a bit cramped, but he should just about be able to take off, at least. You need to test his waterproofing, too. Those feathers on the mended wing have taken quite a bashing with all that strapping up. Give him a tub of water to splash around in and check that the water runs off the wing okay."

They lifted the great bird into his box and packed down the lid.

"Well done!" said the vet. He shook Tony firmly by the hand as if he was presenting him with a prize or something. Clare caught Tony's eye and they smiled at each other.

Mr Craven's house was on a steep slope near the golf course. He had a long garden full of seed frames and water butts and neat rows of potato plants. Against the side of the house there was a wooden shed with fine mesh across the front and there were finches and budgerigars flying backwards and forwards inside.

Tony stood with his face pressed against the mesh, watching an orange bird flitting from perch to perch. Its beak was tiny and its miniature wings twitched in a movement that was more like blinking than flapping.

"They're a bit more dainty than your big fella," said Mr Craven, coming and standing beside Tony. Bono's box was in the middle of the path. He was battering his newly freed wings against the sides and straining the piece of string that held the lid in place.

"He looks ready for the off," said Clare.

"Well ... shall we go for it?" Mr Craven asked, with an eager grin.

The garage was empty, apart from some step-ladders and a bicycle. They carried Bono's box into the middle of the concrete floor and Tony spread some newspaper round it. Mr Craven dragged an old tin bath in from the garden and

Clare filled it with water from the hosepipe.

"What if he can't do it any more?" said Tony, suddenly apprehensive, as they struggled to untie the knotted string. It hadn't really crossed his mind that Bono might not fly again, that he might not survive once he was released. What if it had all been a waste of time?

"He'll be fine – he's raring to go – listen to him!"

Mr Craven flicked open a penknife and cut the string. The lid flew open and Bono raised himself up on his pink legs, shrieking loudly and throwing back his head.

They stepped back as he hopped from the box and walked across the paper, wings stretched out, strutting, like a wrestler flexing his biceps.

"He's more likely to fly if we go outside – we can watch him through the window," said Mr Craven.

It was several minutes before Bono flew. Tony watched him in silence, through the pane of glass, willing him to rise off the ground each time he hopped, or ran, or flapped his wings. He let out a triumphant "Yeah!" as the bird finally sprang into the air and flew the length of the garage. Tony's face was flushed with emotion. He turned round and spontaneously kissed the top of Clare's head. Mr Craven saw, and smiled to himself. He left them looking through the window and went into the house. Clare squeezed Tony's hand.

"You did it!" she said with a beaming smile.

"We'll never catch him now!" said Tony, laughing.

Mr Craven came back with some glasses of Coke and a packet of biscuits.

"How's he doing?" he asked, peering in.

"He's preening himself," said Tony.

Bono was perched on the edge of the water tub, teasing at his wing feathers with his beak. Drops of moisture were glistening on his silver back where he'd plunged into the water.

"He's given up on the flying," said Clare. "He looked really annoyed that there wasn't more space!"

"Poor old beggar," said Mr Craven, brushing biscuit crumbs off his beard. "I think we're going to have to bribe him back into that box. Does he like bacon?"

There was no one at home when they got back to the vicarage. Clare was in fits and giggles.

"Did you see that bloke's face when he heard the box squawk in the luggage rack?" she said.

"I wonder what he thought was in there," Tony laughed.

"He'll probably go home and phone the RSPCA and report us!"

"Will you come and visit me in prison?"

They carried the box carefully in at the back

door and lifted it into Bono's pen.

"I suppose we'll have to keep this door shut all the time, now he can fly out – I don't think Grandma would like to find him in her bath!" Tony snorted with laughter.

"Or raiding the fridge!" said Clare, joining in the joke.

Tony felt very happy. "Coffee?" he said. Clare nodded. He pressed the switch on the kettle.

"And music ..." he said, disappearing into the lounge.

"Turn it up!" shouted Clare, as the music started and she heard what it was. Tony turned the volume up as far as it would go and danced raunchily back into the kitchen, waggling his plastercast from side to side.

"Whoo! Fun-ky!" said Clare, joining in. As they jigged round the kitchen, clapping and swaying, they both sang along noisily.

Tony had his back to the door as his dad and grandma came in, but the look on Clare's face made him turn round. Grandma was crying. She was clutching a carrier bag and dabbing at her nose with a hanky. Her eyes were ringed with red. Clare ran into the lounge and switched off the record player. Tony stood looking at his dad's pale and worried face.

"Sorry, Dad," he said quietly.

Chapter 17

There was a dismal silence in the house. Tony was spreading clean sheets of newspaper in Bono's pen and raking out dirty straw. Bono was sitting sulking in the open box, resentful at being confined again. Clare had gone home, and the morning's euphoria had evaporated into gloom.

Tony heard his dad talking on the telephone. From the annexe he could make out only the rise and fall of his voice – no words – so he went into the kitchen and hovered behind the door, where he could hear more clearly. His dad had said little to him since they came back – only that his mum was very poorly. Tony hated being kept in the dark, hated not knowing what was going on, not being told things straight. He felt guilty too –

guilty that he'd enjoyed being with Clare so much
– just guilty.

He heard his dad say "pneumonia" and then
something about them "stopping treating her …
so it will run its course …" His dad's voice
sounded flat, matter-of-fact. Tony tried to make
sense of what he was saying, tried to guess at the
other half of the conversation. What did "run its
course" mean? Was he saying they'd stopped
trying to make his mum get better? Did that mean
this was it?

His dad continued, calm and unemotional.
Tony froze as he heard his words … "just waiting
… not long now … it will be a great blessing …"
He couldn't listen any more. He wanted to kick
the door open and shout, to wrench the telephone
receiver from his father's hand and dash it to the
floor.

Instead, he grabbed his coat and went out,
slamming the back door behind him.

It was weeks since he'd been down on the
beach. He wasn't meant to get the plaster wet or
dirty, but he didn't care, right now. He stumbled
down the cliff path, dragging the heavy cast across
sand and mud. In the middle of the stretch of
beach there were some rocks, washed flat by the
tide, slimed with green, and full of deep pools.
Tony headed for them and scrambled on to the
highest, a knot of red sandstone, crusted with

winkle shells and draped with twisted black sea-weed – the kind with little puffy bits that you can pop with your thumb.

The tide was coming in, bashing at the rocks underneath him. He picked up a handful of pebbles and hurled them at the waves in rapid succession, like machine-gun fire.

He felt as though he would explode with anger. How could his dad be so callous about his mum, so unmoved by it all? He sounded as though he actually wanted her to die, as though he was just waiting ... and to discuss her in a voice that sounded like he was fixing up a church coffee morning ...

Tony smashed a piece of slate against the rock as he thought of his father. He felt as though he hated him. How dare he let them stop giving her treatment ... and how dare he talk about "Blessings" for God's sake!

Tony looked up at the high cliff behind where he sat. There, crouched on the top, black and brooding, was the steeple of the church. It looked like a grotesque bird, hunched and waiting to swoop – like the stone eagles on the tombstones in the churchyard that had haunted Tony as a child.

What sort of God was there? What sort of God let people die of horrible diseases? What God at all?

Tony tore a piece of leathery seaweed from the

rock and wrapped it round his hand. He pulled it tight and tugged at his fingers until it hurt him and made his knuckles sore. His eyes were full of tears – hot and stinging and salty like the drips of spray that were splashing up from the waves.

He sat there for a long time, letting the tears run down his face, and letting the coming and going of the water soothe his mind into a sober calm.

When he got back his dad was in the garden, turning over sticky lumps of earth with a spade. Tony went into the house and put the kettle on. The house was quiet – his grandma must be in bed. He made tea and took two steaming mugs out to the back door step. His dad came across, without speaking, and sat on the step beside him.

The light was starting to fade. A flock of gulls circled overhead. They sat in silence, hands cupped round the hot mugs, sipping the tea. Tony's face was swollen, and blotchy from crying, and his plastercast was spattered with slimy mud.

Suddenly, as if he had to say it – had to spit it out or else he'd choke – he said, "Mum's going to die, isn't she?"

His dad put his cup down on the step and poked soil from under his finger nails. "Yes," he said, expressionlessly.

Tony swallowed hard. "Have the doctors given up?" His voice sounded cold and bitter.

"It's what she wanted," said his dad, quietly. "She wants them to let her die this time."

Tony felt himself starting to cry again. The words were so final, so absolute, like the rocks on the beach – unflinching, unmoved by the waves battering against them.

He looked at his dad, expecting no emotion on his face, expecting to see a stony blank, a wall of nothing. But, to Tony's amazement, he was crying too. He'd never seen his dad cry before. His eyes were red and screwed tight and his hunched shoulders were shaking uncontrollably. Tony leaned his weight against him and with a loud tortured sob his dad put his arm around him and clasped him tight.

They sat for what seemed like an age, locked together in the evening half light. Above them, in the shadow of the steeple, the gulls were circling, and far below, at the base of the cliffs, the sea was licking the sand and roaring softly.

Chapter 18

The following day was Palm Sunday. Reg Bennett strode energetically down the centre of the church, brandishing a branch above his head and shouting, "Hosanna!"

Behind him the Sunday School marched in a procession, waving plumes of green crêpe paper and cardboard palm leaves.

"Ride on, ride on in Majesty …" they sang, as a small boy wobbled precariously on the backs of two people draped in a grey blanket with large donkey's ears pinned on the sides. The church was more full than usual, with lots of mums and dads smiling indulgently at their children, decked out in dressing-gowns with tea towels tied on their heads.

Tony felt uncomfortable amid the cheering and the hearty singing. The giggling children and the noisy waving seemed jangling and inappropriate. He sat towards the back, staring at the floor, wishing he hadn't come. Beside him in the pew his grandma fidgeted with a handkerchief and crossed and uncrossed her ankles.

As the procession reached the front of the building, the children queued up while Tony's dad gave each of them a little cross made out of plaited palm leaves. He was smiling bravely, trying to enter into the spirit of it: but as he climbed the steps into the pulpit to speak, his face looked grim and haggard. Tony watched him and thought how vulnerable he looked …

After yesterday he felt a new sympathy for him. How must it feel to look out over the rows of faces all staring at you – all expecting you to say something – to say the right thing? Everyone expected him to cope, to be strong – an example of strength. Even Tony – however unconsciously – demanded that of him. Maybe that was the problem. Maybe the burden of coping, like a heavy suit of armour, had imprisoned the real him, the him that Tony longed to know. Tony watched as he took a deep breath and began to talk. There were no jokes, no funny stories to break the ice, no light-hearted anecdotes. He was talking about Jesus.

"As he rode into Jerusalem on that first Palm Sunday ..." Tony heard him say, "he heard the cheers and the celebrations ... but *he knew* that he was facing death ... he knew he was going there, to die ..."

Tony bit his lip and stared hard at the polished wood of the pew in front of him. His dad's voice sounded crackly, thin – as though he might break down, might not be able to finish what he was saying. Beside him, Tony could hear his grandma sniffing, dabbing at her nose with the hanky.

He looked up at the crucifix, high on the wall ahead, its arms stretched out in agony and its marble hands bleeding. The figure of Christ was chiselled from white stone. It looked smooth and cold, like wax. Tony remembered what Clare had said about her grandma looking like a waxwork. He thought he was going to be sick. Clutching his coat, he shuffled along the pew and rushed out of the back door into the sunlight.

Outside the air was warm and the sea was all blue and sparkly.

At Gary's house, Gary's mum was making Yorkshire puddings. She was wearing her pink slippers and there was a delicious smell of roasting dinner in the kitchen.

"Come in, love," she said, wiping her hands on a towel. She smiled at Tony – a warm, cosy smile.

"You look a bit pale, love. You all right?" she asked. Tony nodded. He felt all cold and numb.

"Coffee?" She didn't wait for an answer. "They're in there – glued to the box – go on in."

Gary and his dad were sitting with their feet up watching some football on the television. Gary's dad winked at Tony.

"You all right, kid?" he said, taking a swig from a can of beer.

"Hi, Tones," said Gary, with a casual nod.

"Is this the World Cup qualifier from the other night?" asked Tony, looking at the screen.

"Yeah, it's a vid. Dad hasn't seen it yet, 'cos he was working. Didn't you see it either?"

Tony shook his head. He'd been at the hospital when it was on and had missed it. Besides, they hadn't had the telly on much since Grandma came because there wasn't much she liked watching.

Tony settled down in front of it, sinking deep into the velvety sofa, grateful for the distraction and the warm, airless room.

"Watch this!" said Gary, suddenly, waving his arms in the air and bouncing up and down in his chair.

"Gary Pallister comes in … look at that pass … tackles the Hungarian guy … out to Platt … in to Shearer … then, look, he shoots … oh bloody brilliant goal … one nil!"

"How many times have you watched this?" said Tony, amused by Gary's in-depth commentary on the moves.

"Loads," said Gary, without turning his eyes away from the screen.

"Now, look at this header by Gary Pallister! God, Tones, no wonder they named him after me … he's ace!" They all laughed.

"Oh, Gascoigne, what d'you call that?" Gary's dad shouted at the set. "Pathetic!" he said, gulping back a mouthful of beer. "He's never been any good since he left Newcastle … biggest mistake he ever made that was …"

Tony smiled to himself. No wonder Gary was so opinionated – his dad was even worse.

"Half-time! Put the kettle on, Mam!" shouted Gary.

"What's Brian Robson doing in the studio?" said Tony. "Isn't he playing?"

"Nah," said Gary's dad. "He's injured again, isn't he?"

"He's always flipping injured," said Gary. "Worse than Tony Sharp!" Gary kicked Tony's plaster cast and laughed.

"Just you wait," said Tony. "It's coming off next week – I'll be back!"

"Yeah, just in time for the cricket season!" Gary jumped up and turned the sound down on the television.

"Hey, wait till I tell you about last night, Tones," he said. He paused, grinning broadly, waiting for Tony to quiz him.

"Well, go on then … ask me what happened …" he said, getting no reaction from Tony. Tony sighed and rolled his eyes heavenward then, with mock eagerness, he asked, "What happened last night, Gary?"

Gary was straight in. "I scored in a big way, Tones! Sharon Johnson … down the Youth Club Disco … wait till you hear about it … it'll make you flipping green!"

"Sure Gary," said Tony, shrugging his shoulders and grinning.

He pictured Sharon, pouting and sulky looking. She always wore lots of black make-up round her eyes and her hair was sort of frothed up with blonde streaks in it. She was quite pretty, Tony thought, but in an artificial, glossy sort of way – not like Clare.

"You should have seen her, Tones. She looked flipping gorgeous – dead tight jeans, with a rip across the knee, and this slinky T-shirt thing …"

Tony's eyes glazed over as Gary began to talk. He was thinking about Clare, standing looking into the pond in the park, droplets of drizzle in her hair.

"… She was with this girl in the Sixth Form,

right, and all the time they were dancing, they were like looking over at me, and giggling and nudging each other, you know – making it really obvious that she fancied me ..."

Tony smirked. "They might just have thought you were dancing like a right wally!" he said.

Gary's dad looked over his paper and laughed. "Or they'd noticed you were flying at half mast!"

"Ha-ha, Dad!" said Gary, pulling a long-suffering face. "You're both just jealous!"

Gary's dad winked at Tony and sank back down behind the *News of the World*.

"So, did you go over and ask her to dance, then?" Tony tried to sound interested in Gary's story, but really he was thinking of Clare. He was glad things between them were still a secret – Danny Mason didn't seem to have told anyone he'd seen them walking along the seafront. Tony remembered the way she'd taken his arm in the park. He felt her fingers stroking his sleeve ...

"... Nah, but wait till you hear this ... just before the last record, her friend came over and said, 'Sharon wants to go out with you and she wants to know if you'll walk her home ...' and the rest ... well, it's Adults Only stuff, Tones ... not for your tender ears ... but it was red hot, I'm telling you … she couldn't get enough of me!"

"The second half's starting, Gary," said Tony, nodding at the telly. Gary turned the volume back up as his mum came in with a tray of coffee. Tony sank down in the warm sofa. He thought of Clare gently kissing him by the railings on the promenade – her warm breath on his mouth, and the smell of peppermint, and the touch of her fingers on his cheek. Just remembering it gave him a kind of pleasure that was almost pain. He wondered if this was what being in love felt like.

"Oh, look at that … FOUL, ref, surely!" shouted Gary. "Andy Cole should've got a penalty there …"

"Biased Belgian git!" said his dad, as the game continued. Tony pressed his head back into the velvety cushions and drank his coffee. Suddenly, football seemed strangely un-important.

Chapter 19

"You go on up, and we'll join you soon – I think she'd like to see you on your own." Tony's dad laid his hand on his shoulder. Tony smiled and nodded. He watched as his dad and his grandma walked along the polished white corridor and out into the hospital grounds.

His mum's room was full of flowers and sunlight was streaming in through the parted blinds. She lay, propped up on piles of white pillows, covered only in a thin sheet. A nurse was lifting her arms, wiping her skin with a wet sponge.

"I'll be only a few minutes," she said to Tony, "this is just to cool your mum down. Her temperature's very high."

Tony sat on a chair beside the bed. His mum

craned her head round very slowly and mouthed "Hi". Tony grinned and raised his hand in a Red Indian salute. "How!" he said. He thought how thin she looked – her legs were like sticks, blue and brittle-looking. The nurse ran a wet cloth across his mum's face. Her skin looked flaky and yellowed, like old parchment.

"All right then, love," the nurse said, tucking the sheet in round her, "I'll leave you alone now. Do you want a cup of tea, Tony?"

The door clicked shut. Tony pulled his chair round so that his mum was facing him, and rested his cast on the edge of the bed.

"How's … your … leg?" she said slowly. She could hardly talk. Her voice was thick and hoarse, as though her throat was closing up. It was like lip reading.

"I think it's just about better." Tony spoke quickly, filling the room with chatter. There was so much he wanted to say.

"I've to come to outpatients on Wednesday for them to take the plaster off … it feels like it's healed okay … I can't wait to get rid of it … hopefully I'll be back in the team for the last few games of the season – there are a couple of 'Friendlies' in the holidays – if I haven't lost my touch … And I can start doing my paper round again, which is good because I'm skint!"

His mum listened. She tried to nod and smile,

but every movement took an enormous effort. "How's ... Bono?" she mouthed.

Tony thought of Saturday morning. He remembered the thrill of watching through the garage window, his nose pressed against the glass, as Bono flexed his wings. And he remembered Clare squeezing his hand, sharing his excitement.

"He flew yesterday!" he said, triumphantly. Tony stretched out his arms and imitated Bono, gliding across the garage.

"Just a few yards, but he used the wing. The vet seemed to think it had mended perfectly. He's even more bad-tempered than usual though – now that the bandage is off! Somehow I don't think he'll miss me much once he's back in the wild!"

Tony laughed. He looked into his mum's face. Her eyes had a kind of faraway look, as though she was there, but not quite there – moving on another plane. She looked serious, lost in thought.

She turned her head and raised her hand a few inches off the bed, gesturing to the cabinet beside her bed.

"Do you want something?" Tony jumped up, scanning the cluttered shelf.

"A drink?" He reached out for the jug of water. She rolled her head slowly from side to side.

"Eagle," she murmured.

The framed picture was standing between a box

of tissues and some grapes. Tony reached out and took it. He tried to press it into her hands but she pushed it away and said, in a jerky whisper,

"I … want … you … to … have … it …"

Tony fingered the silver frame and looked at the golden bird, flying over the forest of pine trees. He remembered drawing it, sat hunched over an encyclopaedia in his bedroom, trying to get the plumage right, and the shape of the beak. He'd done a good job. He remembered his mum's face when he'd helped her tear the Christmas paper off it. She'd asked him to hold it close to her face so she could see it clearly, take it all in. Her eyes had been full of tears.

Tony slipped it into the pocket of his coat. He felt himself choking with tears. There were so many things he'd wanted to say to his mum and had never been able to. Now he felt urgent, as though time was slipping through his fingers like grains of sand. He took hold of her hand. It was cold. He thought of the marble saint in the cathedral and gripped tight. His eyes were stinging with tears, hot and prickling, welling up against his eyelids like a dam about to burst.

"I love you, Mum …" he blurted out. Then he buried his face in her sheet and sobbed. When he looked up her face was wet. He pulled a wodge of tissues from the box and mopped her cheeks and the dribbles that were coursing down her chin.

She smiled weakly, painfully. Tony took another tissue and blew his nose very noisily.

"Fog on the river!" he said, as he trumpeted into the handkerchief. She tried to laugh.

The door opened. Dad and Grandma stood in the doorway with a tray of tea that the nurse had just pressed into their hands. Tony sniffed and stood up.

"I'll pass on the tea, thanks, Dad. Do you mind if I go for a walk? I'll meet you back at the car ..."

There was a park across the road from the hospital with some flower beds and an empty paddling pool. Here and there, there were clumps of crocuses, plump and egg yellow. Tony sat on a swing. The afternoon sun was quite warm. He unbuttoned his coat.

He watched a little boy in red wellies splash through a muddy puddle and scramble, laughing, up the wooden steps of the slide.

"Look, Mummy! I'm high!" he said, standing on the top, stretching his tiny fingers up to the sky. He plopped to his bottom and slid down, arms flailing. His mother scooped him up as he reached the ground and threw him up in the air, with a toss of her head.

"Again!" he shouted with delight. "Do again!"

Tony put his hands in his pockets. He felt the shape of the picture frame and ran his thumb around the edge of it. Taking it out, he held it on his knees, tracing his fingers across the glass, following the course of the outstretched bird. As he rocked gently backwards and forwards, scuffing his feet on the tarmac and listening to the creaking of the unoiled swing, he thought of the words he knew so well – the words his mum loved so much.

"He gives strength to the weary ... They will soar on wings like eagles, they will run and not grow weary, they will walk and not be faint ..."

Chapter 20

It was just starting to get light. Pale strands of yellow were poking through the blinds and glimmering on the white sheet. There was an intense quiet in the room, broken only by slow, rasping intakes of breath – well spaced out and getting less and less frequent.

Tony blinked hard to stop his eyelids from falling shut and stifled a yawn. The cuffs of his pyjama jacket were poking out from under his jumper and his hair was ruffled and unkempt. He looked at his dad, sitting opposite him, leaning forward, elbows on knees, his folded hands resting on the crumpled sheet. His eyes were shut and his head bowed forward as though he was praying.

Tony's grandma was beside him – pale without her make-up. She sat, motionless, staring at the dimly lit bed.

They'd been there for what seemed like hours. Just waiting. A clock ticked on the wall. Tony was counting the seconds, timing the gaps between breaths.

His mum was lying flat, her hands clasped together on top of the covers. She could no longer talk, and her eyes, wide and sunk deep in their sockets, were staring at the ceiling. Tony found it hard to look at her. She hardly blinked and her eyes looked as though they were seeing something far, far away – something he could only guess at. The rhythmic ticking throbbed in Tony's head.

"Forty three, forty four, forty five …" He glanced at the clock. It was ten to eight. She had stopped breathing.

They all sat, frozen, waiting for another rasp, eyes fixed on the motionless sheet, willing another movement. There was an aching silence. The nurse sitting by the door stepped forward and gently felt his mum's wrist. Then she pressed her eyelids shut and left the room.

Tony felt numb. He couldn't speak. He fumbled with the sleeves of his sweater and cleared his throat.

His dad bent forward and placed his face on his wife's arm. His eyes were clenched shut, his face twisted up with pain. It was as though a mask, concealing years of hurting, and disappointment, and lost opportunity, was being ripped off and scrunched up like worthless paper.

"Alison," he said softly, as he kissed her arm, "Alison ..."

It shocked Tony to hear him speak her name with such tenderness. The girl in the floppy sun-hat flashed through his mind and he heard her laugh, warm and musical. His dad was crumpled by the bedside, doubled up as though in terrible pain and howling like a baby. Tony's throat was aching. Part of him wanted to run from the room – to be alone – but he couldn't take his eyes off this shaking, helpless figure that was his father. He felt himself – as if motivated by some force from outside him – reach out and grasp the fingers that clawed at the cold sheet. His father opened his hand and enfolded Tony's fingers in his. He gripped them in wild desperation, crushing them tightly as he sobbed into the bedclothes.

It was fully light now. The drive home from the hospital had passed without Tony seeming to notice it. He felt blinded by his intent, numbed by a kind of hope that burned into him and drove him on.

He walked across the sand holding the wriggling bird tightly against his chest. Bono was straining to be free, thrashing his head from side to side and squawking. Tony gripped the bird's beak in the suede gloves and pressed his elbows together, pinning the great wings against Bono's silvery body …

There was a strong wind coming off the sea. Tony braced himself against it and ploughed towards the waves. He was still in his pyjamas with his parka buttoned fast over the top.

The sea was grey – stormy, and thick with white foam. It thundered against the breakwater.

As he reached the water's edge, Tony looked up. The sky was streaked with cloud, plumes of grey moving quickly, racing overhead. Far out beyond the end of the pier, a fishing boat was tossing in the swell, gulls swarming and circling in its wake, diving in and out of the trail of foam.

Tony closed his eyes. He leaned into the wind, feeling its power, and feeling its wetness slapping against his face. His mind was racing. His head was full of dreamlike images. It was as if the clouds were splitting apart and the banks of drizzling grey seemed to dissolve into a turquoise brightness. Tony could see mountains far below him – sharp, jagged peaks, aglow with orange shadows. There was a flash of silver, a lake, fringed with prickly trees, pressing close to the water's edge – tall evergreens.

He felt as if he was skimming across the water,

glimpsing a white reflection, a soft underbelly, flecked and feathered, with limbs stretched out. He could feel the wind carrying him upwards. The light was changing – now blue, now purple, now an incandescent white.

Tony crouched low, feeling the power of the outstretched arms. His trembling fingers caressed thick feathers, smooth and waxy – but hardening as he touched them, hardening to marble, cold and white. He felt the cool hardness of the milky crucifix, glinting on the church wall, and then flesh – warm and muscular and pulsating with life. The sky was glowing red. Trailing below him the white sheet, crumpled and shroudlike, caught the light like a bank of flames, dancing on the wind …

Tony took a deep breath and opened his eyes, staring out at the grey sea. He could feel Bono's pulse, pounding against his chest. The time was right, now.

As the waves lapped his feet, he flung wide his arms and the bird thrashed its wings and broke free. Tony's dad was watching from the top of the cliff path. He saw the gull dart over the foam and circle across the bay, swooping low over the water, testing its strength. Then it landed on the wet sand a few yards from where Tony was standing, drenched in spray.

"Go on, Bono! You're free!" Tony yelled as the

bird stretched its wings out on the sand and blinked at him. It sat very still, staring.

He ran towards it, screaming, "Go on, fly, for God's sake!"

The bird hopped a few paces, wings spread, and then lunged forward, screaming and flapping, battling into the wind, soaring out over the rocks, over the pier – out to the fishing boat.

Tony stood on the beach, watching, his arms still outstretched, leaning into the wind.

"You can fly," he whispered.

Bono's familiar shape merged with the other gulls – flecks of white, darting and swooping in the pale sky. Tony fixed his eyes on the bird until he could barely make him out.

His face was turned upwards. Heavy drops of rain were starting to fall, streaming down his cheeks.

"You can fly," he said again.

As he spoke, he caught sight of his father standing at the top of the slope, tiny against the steep cliff and the towering steeple. Tony could barely make him out, but as he looked he saw him raise his arm and wave. It was a subdued wave, hesitant and uncertain.

Tony was strangely glad to see him and as he lifted his hand to wave back he yelled out at the top of his voice, "He can fly! Dad, he can fly! Fly like an eagle!"